Simon Raven ~~ucated at Charterhouse an~ he read Classics. Afterwa~ ire Light Infantry. In 1957 he resigned his commission ~~ turned to book-reviewing. His first novel, *The Feathers of Death*, brought instant recognition and his popular *First-born of Egypt* series encompasses seven volumes. His TV and radio plays, of which *Royal Foundation* is the best known, are classics. He also wrote the scripts for the *Pallisers* series and *Edward and Mrs Simpson*.

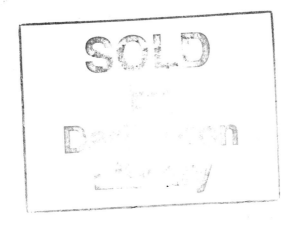

SIMON RAVEN

Blood of My Bone
THE FIRST-BORN OF EGYPT: VOLUME V

HOUSE OF
STRATUS

This edition published in 2001 by House of Stratus, an imprint of
Stratus Books Ltd., 21 Beeching Park, Kelly Bray,
Cornwall, PL17 8QS, UK.

www.houseofstratus.com

Typeset, printed and bound by House of Stratus.

A catalogue record for this book is available from the British Library
and the Library of Congress.

ISBN 1-84232-176-5

Meantime the black blood gushed in a pool about the navel of Adonis, and his breast, that had once been as white as snow, was made crimson by the flux from his thighs.

Bion's *Lament for Adonis*, 11.25-27
Translated by SR

PART ONE

The Death of a Don

And Death the while –
Death with his well-worn, lean, professional smile,
Death in his threadbare working trim –
Comes to your bedside unannounced and bland,
And with expert, inevitable hand
Feels at your windpipe, fingers you in the lung,
Or flicks the clot well into the labouring heart:
Thus signifying unto old and young,
However hard of mouth or wild of whim,
'Tis time – 'tis time by his ancient watch – to part
From books and women and talk and drink and art.
And you go humbly after him
To a mean lodging: on the way
To what or where
Not Death, who is old and very wise, can say:
And you – how should you care
So long as, unreclaimed of hell,
The Wind-Fiend, the insufferable,
Thus vicious and thus patient, sits him down
To the black job of burking London Town?

W E Henley; *London Voluntaries 4, Largo e mesto:*
Poems (1898)

On a day in september, 1981, in the precinct of Lancaster College, Cambridge, a Dominie lay dying.

This was Sir Thomas Llewyllyn, Knt, D. Litt. and Litt. D., the Provost of the College, who had long been ailing in body, mind and spirit: in body, from the delayed effect of youthful excess; in mind, because of the concomitant deterioration of the physical brain that embodied it; and in spirit because he had a great and guilty sorrow, that it was by his order that the Elms of the College Avenue had been destroyed and the nymphs unhoused to wander away to their death. The fact that the removal of the Elms had been a pressing hygienic necessity and no fault whatever of Sir Thomas need not detain us; let us simply note that he was a superstitious and sentimental man despite the former powers of his intellect, and then pass to the scene of his passing.

Gathered round his bed in the Provost's Lodging were his friends: his Private Secretary and chosen companion, Len; Miss Carmilla Salinger, a Fellow of Lancaster and a tutor (kindly mark the small 't' in this instance) in Mediaeval History; Piero Caspar, a recent graduate, with starred first class honours, who had been appointed to a Fellowship of the College a few weeks previously by the Provost's Special Decree; Ivan 'Greco' Barraclough, an Anthropologist who specialized in the inhabitants of the Peloponnese; and Ivan's protégé, untouched by hand or at any rate untouched by the Greco's, Nicos Pandouros, a slow, loyal youth, capable of intelligent thought when allowed the leisure normally refused to him by Barraclough. All these people stood to suffer by the Provost's death; for he was in many degrees their patron, and his demise would mean

3

an end of his patronage. However, it was not of this that they were thinking now. As the Provost lay doped and stertorous along the bed, Carmilla Salinger said, 'The College Matron, Mrs Batch, is getting ready to raise a row. She wants him moved to a Hospital outside. She says that the Resident College Doctor is incompetent to cure anything more serious than warts and chilblains. Since Doctor Grilby is now over ninety, she is, of course, right. But it is still not fitting that the Provost, the Vicar on Earth of our Blessed Founder, King Henry VI, be moved out of the College.'

'Then,' said Greco Barraclough, 'let us call an outside Doctor in.'

'He would say the same as Matron Batch,' said Piero Caspar: 'that Sir Tom must be moved into a Hospital.'

'And is that really so bad?' said Barraclough.

'It is not fitting,' repeated Carmilla: 'Princes must die in their Palaces.'

'Amen,' said Nicos Pandouros. 'Besides, if they once get him into a Hospital, they will keep him alive much longer...to no possible purpose, save to prolong his pain and humiliation.'

'That is exactly what they enjoy doing most,' said Len: 'officiously preserving the lives of once eminent men who now long to die, taking reprisal for the privilege and esteem which they formerly commanded, watching with relish as they dirty themselves like infants and writhe impotently in surgical chairs.'

'They must be prevented,' said Piero. 'Now, this morning Balbo Blakeney came to me and offered a lethal draught, which, he thought, was undetectable. As a trained biochemist, he should know better. No draught is undetectable. But his offer gave me an idea.' His faun-face narrowed and rippled. 'In Sicily we use draughts only when the Doctor is venal. When he is not, we have a song.'

'A song?' murmured Carmilla, smoothing the dark grey trousers along her ample thighs.

4

'A song. Unlike draughts, songs leave no traces in the blood. Yes, Carmilla, a song. A variant on the old Linossong, of which Homer and others speak: part a song of harvest and part farewell to summer.'

The Provost opened his eyes.

'Milo,' he called; 'Milo.'

'He is not here, Provost. He cannot be reached.' The Provost moaned in despair.

'Baby. My Tullia. Baby.'

'Gone, Provost; gone.'

'Sarum? Tullius? Sarum.'

'Gone for ever; gone.'

'*Marius*?'

'He is waiting outside, Provost,' said Len. 'Is it your will that he attend you?'

'Bring him.'

Len went to the bedroom door, opened it and beckoned. Marius Stern came in, a rangy fifteen-year-old, with bright green eyes and soft blond hair. He moved to the bed and bowed.

'Here am I, Provost,' he said: 'Marius Stern.'

'I am sorry to have summoned you from your School and your studies,' said the Provost, in a very low but otherwise normal voice.

'I am honoured.'

'Hear me then. You are the son of my wife's sister and of a man, now dead, that was once very dear to me. And this is what I must tell you. There was until recently in your School a boy called Milo Hedley. He has left it now, and will come to this University, though not to this College, in October. This last summer he came here, to my Lodging, and made the time pass pleasantly, for he was an agile, witty, plausible and (in his kind) most charming boy. But others of my friends, those gathered here today, would not suffer him and stayed away from me while he was here. At the time I was sad: now I realize that they

5

were right. Have nothing to do with this boy, Marius: eschew him utterly and shun him.'

'He is a friend of mine, Provost, and has been so for some time.'

'I know, Marius. Nevertheless, eschew him and shun him utterly. He will come often to your School although he has left it; he will come to see you and to see a master there called Raisley Conyngham, whom you also know. From now on you must turn your back on them both. I know that they are striving to enslave and corrupt you, and that this last summer they almost succeeded. So much was clear to me when I came to Canteloupe's house in August, to find my grandson, your cousin Sarum dead. They thought I was an old fool that understood nothing. But I listened here and I listened there, and I learned that, though Sarum had indeed died, as they said, by accident and infortune, he might well, had matters been a few inches or a few seconds more or less, have died by other means with your hand behind them. Eschew Milo Hedley, Marius: shun Raisley Conyngham.'

'Mr Conyngham teaches me. He teaches me to make verses, in Greek and Latin, and to understand the refinements of language.'

'Mr Conyngham teaches you to understand the refinements of Hell. Tread them down and spurn him. For the last time, Marius: eschew Raisley Conyngham and deny Milo Hedley.'

Weakened by his effort, the Provost started to choke and shudder; and then to weep; and then to mutter passage after passage of gibberish, among which could occasionally be distinguished a phrase of true English, either legal or liturgical.

'Our Father hagriches moon gib blongkeep,' jabbered the Provost; 'taken hence to that glabbrock cardigan to that place beechstoon begales buggamill.'

'The College Matron will be here in twenty minutes,' said Carmilla. 'I think – do not you, my friends? – that it is time for Piero to sing his song.'

So Piero sang his song of Linos, of teeming, fruitful September that yet changes the green leaves to yellow. 'Farewell, summer: summer, farewell.' The Provost stretched out one hand, which was taken by Marius; and then the other, which was taken by Carmilla. As the song proceeded, the Provost's eyes closed.

'Farewell, summer: summer, farewell.'

Nicos knelt and started muttering.

'*Kyrie, eleison; Christe, eleison.*'

Len surveyed with satisfaction the way his pink trouser bottoms fitted over the top half of his green suede boots.

Greco Barraclough began to wonder about the Provost's successor.

'*Kyrie, eleison.*'

'Farewell, summer.'

Marius thought: how can I abandon Raisley Conyngham and Milo Hedley, no matter how firmly the old man has charged me on his death bed? For am I not sworn to them, am I not pledged to obedience?

Carmilla thought: we must tell Jeremy Morrison. Any minute now he will be released from his prison in Australia – we must catch him with the news before he leaves it. Then he will come here to pay his duty to this old man, and Theodosia and I can persuade him to go on his journey, the journey on which he must go for his health, his salvation, and his honour.

Marius thought: this hand is dead.

'Farewell, summer: summer, farewell.'

'*Christe, eleison.*'

Carmilla walked with Marius on the back lawn of Lancaster, late in the afternoon.

'We did our best for him,' she said. 'Are you going to do yours?'

'He is dead, Carmilla.'

'As he died, he charged you. Eschew Milo Hedley, he said, and shun Raisley Conyngham. Good advice, by any measure, amounting, in these circumstances, to a command.'

'The commands of dead men have no authority.'

'To obey such commands...their wishes, Marius...is to honour their memory.'

'There will be other ways,' said Marius, 'of honouring the memory of the Provost. As for his commands, his wishes, if you will, they were stated when his mind was unclear – '

' – He was totally clear as to what he was asking you – '

' – But he did not, Carmilla, begin to understand, Carmilla, the affair in which he was presuming to meddle.'

'*Meddle?*'

'Meddle. He was, for a start, trying to come between me and two people whom he did not *understand*, Carmilla, were and still are my greatest friends.'

'Enemies. Greatest enemies.'

'Enemies, Carmilla? One of whom teaches me the Classics in the most stylish and fascinating manner, both of whom protect me from the hazards of life at School and outside it.'

'Both of whom corrupt and entice you among far worse hazards. At your School and outside it.'

'Well,' said Marius, 'Milo, for one, has left School. He will be doing no more corrupting in that precinct.'

'He will return. Often. And Raisley Conyngham is still there.'

'For Christ's sake, Carmilla, what do you expect me to do? Raisley Conyngham has taught me all the most precious things I have ever learnt.'

'Yes. In order to corrupt and abuse you, to have possession of you, to bring you to do the evil deeds which he desires of you.'

'I have done no evil deed. Raisley Conyngham has never possessed me.'

'Not your body. Your spirit. And you have been minded to evil if you have not done it. You were minded to kill Tully Sarum...even though in the end, and through no virtue nor restraint of yours, it was not you that killed him.'

'I was minded to kill him kindly. To spare him the pain and misery of being the abominable thing he was. To bring him peace and absolution. And now I think I should be getting back to School. The Provost asked to speak with me. I came; he has spoken and I have listened politely, as our relative positions required of me; and now he is dead, and that is that. I must get back to School and get on with my work for my O Levels in December.'

'Come with me,' Carmilla said.

She led the way across the lawn towards the West End of the Chapel, turned the North End of Sitwell's Building, and climbed the first staircase along.

'Come in and sit down.'

She went to the telephone and dictated a Foreign Cable, to Jeremy Morrison, c/o The Kelly Gaol in Australia. 'Sir Tom lies dead,' she dictated: 'come.'

Next she apologized to Marius for withdrawing her attention from him, and switched on the electric kettle.

'Tea,' she said. 'You must stay for the Burial.'

'No. I hate funerals. Sir Tom was not a blood relation. I want to go back to School.'

'To Raisley Conyngham.'

'To School.'

'Canteloupe will come to the Burial. And Theodosia.'

'Oh. How is she?'

'If you stay, you will see for yourself.'

'They say she is to bear a girl.'

'Yes, Marius. Canteloupe still wants a son. Next spring you will have to go to Theodosia again. You will like that, won't you? You liked it so much last time...that you came later to me. She had sent you away because she couldn't bear the shame of it any longer…and so you came to me because I was her twin.'

'And you too sent me away.'

'I had a lover: Richard Harbinger.'

'He was a poor thing.'

'A brave explorer.'

'But in other ways, a poor thing. I saw how you despised him. You could have had me too.'

She patted his face, hard. Not quite a slap; a warning.

'Anyway, Harbinger has gone now,' he said. 'Harbinger has gone exploring. Shall you send me away again?'

'No. I shall keep you here…at any rate, until after the Burial of Sir Thomas. Now tea. Tea, tea, tea. Bring the things from that cupboard. Cups, saucers, plates and teaspoons. A knife for each of us. Now it is September we can have muffins again. There are two there. And butter. Gentlemen's Relish, or jam if you prefer.'

'Jam for me, please.'

'Bring the Gentlemen's Relish as well – for me. I shall make the tea if you will toast the muffins by the gas-fire. Milk or lemon?'

'Milk, please.'

'Myself, I like lemon. There is none in the cupboard, but there is a fresh one in the scullery. Could you nip and get it? I'll watch the muffins for you.'

When Marius arrived back with the lemon, she said, 'I think the muffins are done to a turn, Marius. I am spreading some jam for you on this one. You see? Please will you spread some Gentlemen's Relish – I like it rather thick, please – on the other one for me?'

Len and Piero were also having tea, in the Withdrawing-Room of the Provost's Lodging.

'Last meal in the old home,' said Len.

'Not quite.'

Piero settled his club foot on the fender.

'No,' said Len, smirking, a way of his when he disliked the situation in which he found himself. 'No, my dear. Not quite. But the moment the next Provost is elected he'll move in. With a new secretary.'

'Why should he not keep you?'

'Haven't you noticed, darling?' said Len. 'I'm not to everybody's taste. Certainly not to that of the kind of Commissar you'd expect the College Council to elect in these lovely left-wing days of philistine scientists and dripping sociologists. But oddly enough, darling, there *is* just a *tiny* hope that sanity will survive and your old friend Lenikins with it.'

'When will they elect the new Provost?' Piero enquired.

'Ah. That's just it. The statutes provide, in general terms, that a new Provost should be elected *as soon as* the old one is safely buried. The whole College Council is supposed to be locked in the Chapel, immediately after the Burial is over, and not let out until a new man has been chosen. Now then. A lot of the Council are still away, as the Term hasn't started. We'll let 'em know by cable, of course, but most of 'em simply won't make it back in time to vote – even though we've got to wait seven days before we can have the Burial and the Election. Now, darling: Uncle Len here is in charge of sending the cables; so he'll make sure that all the nice people get theirs as promptly as possible and all the nasty old nasties do not.'

'It'll be noticed later. They'll have you up for rigging the thing.'

'Oh no, they won't, dear. You see, a lot of the nasties are busy spouting wind and piss behind the Curtain, or having expensive freebies in the Third World somewhere. Cables take a very long time to get to *those* kind of places, dear, and there's nothing Uncle Len can do about that.'

'But surely…according to the Statutes the Election has to be delayed until all members of the College Council have had time to return.'

'Right, dear. Till the beginning of Full Term, to be precise, on October the twelfth.'

'Then you're talking nonsense,' said Piero screwing up the ugly mouth in his angelic face, 'about locking them into the Chapel to vote right after the Burial. And all this merda about cables – '

' – Not quite nonsense, darling. Those few that are able to attend the Burial *will be locked in*, as a matter of form. And then the Senior Don present will say, "There is no quorum here" – at least three quarters of the Council must be present, you see – and the Second Senior Don will point out that according to the Statutes such Elections must be held during Full Term, and then they'll be unlocked and allowed to disperse.'

'So: close of play until Full Term.'

'Except in one circumstance that has only ever once arisen,' said Len, and blew his nose with a crash into a white handkerchief with purple spots (the College Summer Colours). 'If there is a National or Other Emergency, which makes it necessary that a Provost be at once elected in order to take charge of the College "in Time of Dire Peril", a new Provost may be elected by those Fellows present at the Burial, whenever that may occur and however few of them may be there. The only time this has happened was on the sudden death of Provost Hacklyte in August, 1914. The declaration of War was the pretext. Those who were locked in the Chapel decided in the usual way that the Election must be deferred until Full Term in October, but when they knocked on the door to be let out, they were commanded by the Lord Bishop of Ely, as Visitor of the College, to remain inside and elect a Provost there and then in order that the College might have immediate and authoritative guidance in his *Diebus Belli et Timoris*…a proceeding which provides us with precedent singular but ample.'

'So,' said Piero: 'all you have to do is make sure all the nasties stay away for at least another week, then persuade the Lord Bishop of Ely to declare an Emergency and refuse to let those present at the Burial out of the Chapel until they elect a Provost to our taste?'

'Precisely.'

'Rather a long order, as the chap in Trollope remarks when asked to forge the heiress' signature seventeen times on a fake will?'

'It don't have to be the College Visitor that demands an immediate election. If he is not available, the duty devolves on the Monarch.'

'Splendid. That really eases our problem.'

'Or,' said Len, 'if neither the Visitor nor the Monarch is there to umpire, the decision rests with the Vice-Provost; and if *he* is not available, with the Senior Fellow. He is temporary Head resident within the College, you see; and he is therefore responsible, should a crisis arise, for ensuring that the College has a new and totally effective Provost with the least possible delay. Now then: our Vice-Provost is away in Abyssinia, helping the Communist Government there to find excuses for prolonging the convenient famine of reactionary peasants; but our Senior Fellow *is* in residence at this moment. He is too decrepit not to be. He will be locked into the Chapel with the rest after the Burial, and will hold the key. If he says that there is crisis sufficient to justify the Election of a new Provost *instanter*, then this will be done, even if there is only one other inside the Chapel with him.'

'Who is the Senior Fellow?'

'The Honourable Grantchester FitzMargrave Pough (pronounced Pew), C H, Professor Emeritus of Oriental Geography, at one time celebrated as a mountaineer. Also a vegetarian faddist, but that is by the way. A gentleman of the utmost integrity and distinction. Ideal for the task ahead of him.'

'But surely…the College celebrated his ninety-fifth birthday last March. Decrepit – you said it yourself.'

'I meant physically. He is as sound of mind as ever. Just our man.'

'But you also have to produce a National Crisis or Emergency before you can wheel him into action.'

'National or OTHER Emergency, Piero. I did say so very clearly just now. You leave that to me.'

'With the greatest of pleasure.'

'Now then, the lists. Our tables, Piero; meet it is we set a few things down. First, friends who will want a civilized Provost and not some ghastly Gauleiter of the People: Balbo Blakeney, who is staying in Wiltshire with Canteloupe and is easily summoned; Ivor Winstanley, here in College; Jacquiz Helmutt, at his Manor near Royston, only ten miles away; Lord Burgo Gaviston…'

Raisley Conyngham telephoned from Marius' School at Farncombe to say that it was high time Marius returned there.

'I think,' said Len, who was taking the call, 'that he intends to stay until after Provost Llewyllyn's Burial.'

'But that is still nearly a week away,' said Raisley, who knew the customs of Lancaster College (and those of every other, come to that) as accurately as if it had been his own. 'Kindly tell Marius Stern that we expect him back tomorrow.'

'We?'

'Those responsible for him.'

'He tells me,' said Len, 'that he has already obtained the permission of his Housemaster – backed by the approval of your Headmaster – to stay on here until the day after the Provost's Burial.'

'I am speaking as his Tutor. Whatever his Housemaster or the Headmaster may say, Marius' studies – those in which I am coaching him – may suffer seriously if he loiters about in Cambridge.'

'He is not loitering about. He is using his time very well. He is being supervised, you might say, by a distinguished Fellow of the College, Miss Carmilla Salinger.'

'Can I speak to Marius?'

'No. He has gone with Miss Salinger to visit Ely Cathedral.'

There was an ill-tempered click at the other end. So, thought Len as he put down the receiver, Raisley is bothered. He wants his boy back before the angels of light get to work on him. Next thing we know we'll have Master Milo Hedley the Messenger Boy round here to serve Marius with Raisley's writ. That cute little number certainly has them all hassling.

In Bishop Alcocke's Chantry in Ely Cathedral, Carmilla said to Marius, 'I came here once with Jeremy Morrison. Come behind that screen and I'll show you what happened there.'

That evening, at about six-thirty, Milo Hedley came to the front door of the Provost's Lodging. He had chosen a bad time. As he was about to ring the bell, the door opened and six of the College Porters carried Tom out in his coffin. They were taking him to the College Chapel, to the Chantry of the Blessed Founder, where he would remain until his Burial. Following the coffin were Len, Carmilla, Piero Caspar, Greco Barraclough, Nicos Pandouros, and other friends of Sir Thomas, including Balbo Blakeney, the biochemist, and Ivor Winstanley, the Ciceronian. Sir Jacquiz Helmutt was also there, with his appetizing wife, Marigold, and their two beautiful twin children, a girl and a boy, who had the faces of ten-year-olds and the limbs of finely built adolescents. Marius was at the rear of the procession. Milo hooked on to him.

'Raisley telephoned me,' Milo said to Marius. 'I always let him know where I am, you see, now that I've left School.'

'And where were you?'

'Not very far away, as I am already here. He wants you back at once. Tomorrow.'

The coffin swayed along the Colonnade under the Library and on to the Great Lawn.

'Why does Raisley want me back so quickly?'

'He don't care for the company you're keeping,' Milo Hedley said. 'He doesn't want you to get any silly ideas.'

'He's not usually so…so crude as this. Ringing up the Provost's Lodging and demanding my return. Then calling you out and sending you along like a running fag.'

'Watch your tongue, little Marius; Marius the Egyptian.'

The coffin was about to enter the West Door, which had been thrown open in Provost Llewyllyn's honour, not so much because he had been Provost but because he had been the Avatar on earth of the Blessed King Henry VI, Founder of the College.

'You can't come in,' said Marius to Milo. 'You have no business here.'

'Why not? I was the guest and friend of the Provost last August. We got on very well.' They stepped through the West Door side by side. 'Now then, little Marius; what you have to remember is this: the reason why Raisley is being so crude, as you put it, or so anxious for your welfare, as I should prefer to put it, is that he is seriously afraid for you. As I reported to Raisley after my stay here during last Long Vacation, this College, absurd as it is, a ragbag of reaction on the one hand and lunatic revolution on the other, plagued by incompetence, senility, fanaticism, intrigue, atrophy and casual lust, is nevertheless rather a decent kind of place. Not the kind of place that approves of the kind of training, in social and moral deployment, that Raisley is dishing out to you. He is afraid that time spent here will blunt your enthusiasm for his instruction. He is sure enough of this to employ crude and unsubtle methods, if such are necessary to bring you back to him.'

'I am promised to him,' said Marius, 'to him and to you. Is that not enough?'

The coffin had now been carried into the Founder's Chantry and laid on a catafalque; those that had followed it were crowding in round it. Marius and Milo did not follow them. Through the tracery of the screen (which reminded him slightly of the screen in Bishop Alcocke's Chantry at Ely) Marius could see the marble figure of a pensive and graceful little boy, who was seated with his flanks extended away to his right and his head and neck arched to the left, as if to look down into a pit or a pond. Hylas, thought Marius: the Monument of Canteloupe's son, Sarum of Old Sarum, which the Provost, being the dead boy's grandfather, had caused to be set up in the Chantry only a few weeks before his own death. Now he could lie by his grandson's image, until his body was interred, alongside Sarum's, in the Crypt.

There was a low chanting of Choristers and Choral Scholars. No organ music.

'*Kyrie, eleison.*'

'I am promised,' repeated Marius. 'And if there is anything at all which might make me renounce that promise, it is this shabby evidence of Raisley Conyngham's mistrust.'

'He has a lot on his mind. Captain Lamprey is drinking deep down at Ullacote. Jenny the Stable Lass has left, just disappeared without notice.'

'I gathered from...somebody I know down there, an old Aunt of Palairet's...that the stable was in trouble. And there is another thing, Milo. Mr Conyngham is no longer so kindly regarded at School as he was. This is not an age which much approves of rich schoolmasters that keep strings of racehorses. The Headmaster is conscious of public moods. He realizes, I think, that even upper-class parents are liable to be dubious about Raisley the millionaire bachelor with the swish estate and the private trainer. Nothing wrong with any of these things taken separately. But the combination – not one to recommend itself to those who are sincere about current ideas of education, even of public school education. Raisley is a classical scholar and a civilized man: there is not enough *technology* about him to suit modern notions. Raisley is non-productive.'

'Quite so, Marius. So you understand that he may be feeling nervous.'

'He should not show it as he just has done.'

'KYRIE, ELEISON.'

'Even so, you will be true?'

'I promised him.'

'Then so I shall tell him. He won't, I think, bother you again between now and the Burial. Enjoy your stay in Lancaster. I shall now leave you to the mummery.'

When Milo had gone, Marius joined the crowd in the Founder's Chantry. The two beautiful Helmutt twins turned to look at him. They did not smile in greeting nor frown in deprecation nor blink in puzzlement. They did not move a single muscle in their faces. They simply looked straight at Marius, until the chanting ceased and the party began to disperse through the candlelit Chapel and out into the dusk that crept over the Great Lawn.

After a day or two Carmilla became more serious in her attentions to Marius. Although he still had the impression that he was given sweets to keep him happy, these were no longer just tossed at him as though they were a temporary bribe to hang about the place and were no longer of merely frivolous and casual confection. They were carefully and deliberately presented to him and were of high quality and subtle flavour. Clearly (thought Marius) Carmilla was becoming interested: she was no longer simply seeking to detain him until the Provost's Burial but was developing an insight into his sexual skills and proclivities, which provoked her to specific utterances of appreciation and gratitude. This will continue, thought Marius. Even though he must return to School after the Burial and could not hope to see Carmilla for some time, this would last – and last the longer for the affection which both of them felt at another level, the desire to understand and protect.

Marius knew clearly why Raisley Conyngham had been so anxious to keep him from the Provost's Burial. It was for the same reason as that which had prompted him to prevent Marius' attendance at the Senior Usher's Funeral the previous summer. Raisley was afraid lest the celebration of a life concluded with honour as well as success, and the restrained mourning for a kind and moderate man of great gifts and selfless principle (as the Provost had once been, and had remained, in a sense, until the end) would weaken the appeal of the career which Raisley himself was proposing to Marius, a career of stealthy attachment of power through moral and intellectual manipulation of the innocence and weaknesses of other human beings. In a word, the Provost, for all the vices of his youth and failures of his maturity, stood for decency, he stood for hard work (drudgery when necessary) and fair practice; whereas Raisley stood for mental trickery and spiritual fraud. He, Marius, was being twisted and trained by Raisley into a life of just such trickery. Why, then, did he not rebel against this, as he had seen his friend, Tessa Malcolm, rebel and as the Provost on his death bed had urged him? Because he had promised himself to Raisley Conyngham. And why had he done this? Because he loved, he adored the *persona* (rather than the person) of Raisley Conyngham, was also fascinated by his partner, Milo Hedley, and (last but not least) had a strong taste for the intimate and enticing processes of intrigue to which they were introducing him.

In the end, Marius supposed, there would have to be a choice. Whatever promises he had made to Raisley and Milo (and surely, time, chance and circumstance had a way of invalidating even the most solemn), sooner or later there would have to be a choice, the oldest choice of all, between the good (Carmilla, Piero, the Provost) and the evil (Canteloupe, Glastonbury and his own tutor, Raisley Conyngham). But for the time being, he told himself, he could surely play the field a little, he could balance the problematic rewards of virtuous endeavour against the likely attractions of whatever exercises in mundane strategy Raisley Conyngham and Milo Hedley might be planning next.

Jeremy Morrison, having been released from Kelly Gaol after serving the agreed period in the agreed conditions, and having been handed Carmilla's cable just before his release, flew from Australia to England and came at once to Carmilla in Cambridge. Carmilla was sitting in her rooms in the early afternoon, with Marius. Jeremy kissed them both.

'Here am I,' he said: 'lovely Carmilla and beautiful Marius.'

'But you are not here for long,' replied Carmilla. 'Thea and I have it all worked out for you. A highly publicized departure on an expedition of great peril and hardship, into the secret places of the world…whence you will return, redeemed from your dishonour, to write a book for us at once authentic and very popular.'

'There are no secret places left in the world,' Jeremy said. His huge round face wobbled above his bulky trunk. He had got no thinner (Carmilla noticed) in prison.

'The mind can make them so,' said Marius.

'Possibly, little Egyptian. But I understand a definite geographical progress is required of me. When do I start,' he said to Carmilla, 'and whither?'

'You leave the fourth day after the Provost's Burial,' said Carmilla, 'to allow time for the required publicity, and you fly to Athens.'

'Athens? I thought I was to be sent somewhere remote.'

'Remote in time. From Athens you will take a boat to Ithaca. Odysseus, his Island. You must know the legend? You read the Classics when you were up here. All that in Homer.'

'How Odysseus went to Troy and returned, after a ten-year voyage, to his faithful wife, to live happily ever after.'

'Ah,' said Carmilla, stretching both her long fine legs before her from where she sat on the sofa, 'but *did* he live happily ever after? There is a further and later legend – that he wearied of his ageing and whining wife and his priggish, clinging son, and set out once more with his companions, this time to the West. To the Isles of the Blessed. To find "the great Achilles whom we knew" and the other heroes of the great days in Ilium. That will be your journey. You will leave Ithaca in a motor boat with a cabin big enough for one man to eat and sleep in, and you will sail West for the Isles of the Blessed. I don't suppose you will find them, in the literal sense, but you must voyage on, first by sea, later, if necessary, on land, always to the West, until you come to a place which you know, in your heart and in your spirit, to be to you what the Isles of the Blessed would have been to Odysseus. Then, and then only, may you return.'

'I can take a friend?'

'One friend. One of you will sleep in the cabin while the other takes the wheel. Turn and turn about. Whom shall you take?'

'I should take Marius here if he were older, but Marius must stay behind and mind his book. Whom else should I take, then, but Fielding Gray? We can write the account of the journey together?'

'Why not?' said Carmilla.

'Mrs Maisie Malcolm won't like it,' said Marius. 'She's getting keener and keener on having Fielding near her. She's just spent a long time with him in his home in Norfolk.'

'Quite long enough they've been down there,' said Carmilla. 'He's finished *The Master Baker*, which is the companion volume to *The Great Grinder*. He needs to get off his arse and move about. He's only in his early fifties, and it's high time he stopped being pampered by that Malcolm woman and went out to spread his mind. Now then, Jeremy: I think you understand the elementary principles of navigation? I remember hearing boastful stories of childhood summers on the Broads and the Norfolk coast.'

'I should be able to manage – up to a point. I was in the Naval Section of the Cadet Corps at School. They taught us to steer by Compass and how to read Admiralty Charts.'

' "All I ask is a Tall Ship," ' said Marius, ' "And a Star to steer Her by." ' For a second his green eyes misted. 'How I wish I could go,' he said.

'Well, you can't,' said Carmilla lightly. And to Jeremy: 'Your guest room is ready for you. Come here at seven-fifteen and we will all go to dinner.'

'In Hall? I hear there have been some nasty changes.'

'*Not* in Hall. Not only have there been nasty changes, but some student committee has forbidden the Servants, on pain of expulsion from their union, to serve meals to the Fellows in residence out of Term. So there won't be any dinner in Hall, Jeremy – for which we may be truly thankful.'

'But if it's all as horrid as you say, presumably you wouldn't go anyway.'

'I might. Like many rich women, I have a mean streak – particularly about entertaining men to meals. So thank your stars for that student committee.'

'Righty hoh, darling. Seven fifteen, then. Coming, Marius?'

'No,' said Carmilla: 'Marius will spend the afternoon here.'

'I say,' said Marius a little later, as he lay in Carmilla's arms and fingered her spine; 'rather a long order – what you've just told Jeremy to do.'

'You seemed keen enough on going yourself, had it been possible.'

'My keenness was theoretical – I was keen just because it wasn't possible. It was a literary exercise, as Mr Conyngham would say.'

'Would he?' said Carmilla tightly. 'Well you were certainly right about one thing. Jeremy's mission is a very long order indeed.'

'Why do you have to be so demanding of him?'

'Because I value his honour. Either he will die, which in view of what has happened would be no bad thing, or he will live to wipe out his disgrace by his endeavour.'

'Do you think Fielding will agree to go?'

'Yes. If only to make up for the way in which he deserted Jeremy when Jeremy was arrested in Australia. Fielding often does that kind of thing, just glides away from his friends when they're in trouble, and then gets very guilty later. He will be guilty now, longing to purge himself, and when Jeremy suggests this trip he will leap at it.'

'But why does Jeremy want him? A flabby middle-aged man,' said Marius, 'and treacherous with it?'

'Time was, not so long ago, when Jeremy appealed to Fielding for his advice on how to mould his destiny. He thought, you see, that Fielding had special skill in controlling his life. He still thinks, perhaps correctly, that Fielding is a *survivor*. It will be the reverse, so to speak, of having a Jonah on board.'

'That didn't work in Australia,' said Marius, paddling his fingers further and further down Carmilla's spine: 'Fielding's presence didn't stop Jeremy from getting into trouble with the Police.'

'I have had a full account from Fielding. Jeremy got into trouble because he wouldn't take Fielding's advice. He has as good as admitted this himself, in letters he wrote me from prison.'

'All right,' said Marius, as his fingers found their destination and stayed there. 'What advice can Fielding possibly offer on this motor boat?'

'Well. (Yes, Marius, yes.) They will, of course, cheat. They will have to. They cannot reasonably be expected to voyage due West over the open sea in a small boat, and if they did they would pretty soon run into obstacles and have to sail round them. So they will follow the ancient Greek method. They will sail always within sight of the shore by day and will put into port at evening. Perhaps this time Jeremy will accept Fielding's advice about how to comport himself when ashore among the locals.'

'You'd have thought Jeremy would have learnt his lesson by now in any case.'

'No doubt he has. But after a time conviction will fade and he will hanker once more to seek the haunts of Eros Pandemos, *videlicet* rough trade. It is then that Fielding's advice and restraint will be needed.'

'Fielding might fancy a piece of rough trade too.'

'In which case, they may have the sense to utilize each other, if only as second best. Yes, Marius: *yes.*'

'But they've never done it together before. Jeremy told me.'

'For Christ's sake, darling Marius, stop being contentious. Yes, Marius: oh, yes, yes.'

In the deconsecrated Chancel of the eleventh-century church in which she lived under the ramparts of St-Bertrand-de-Comminges, Isobel Stern said to her friend Jo-Jo Guiscard:

'According to the last *Times* we had, today is the day that they're burying my poor old brother-in-law, Tom Llewyllyn.'

'What did he really die of? He was only just over fifty.'

'Either,' said Isobel, 'he caught something nasty in his spunky youth, something which was never properly cured and has now come back to reclaim him. *Or* he was worn down and rubbed out by just too much sadness. First his wife, my sister, became an incurable and scandalous lunatic. Then the Elms in Lancaster died, and soon after them his daughter. Then his grandson, Little Tully Sarum. I think, too, that he lost interest. He was so appalled by the futility, conceit and false pretences of modern man, by whom nothing is thought worth thinking, nothing said worth saying, and nothing read whatever, that he just gave up.

'I dreamt of him last night,' Isobel said. 'I dreamt of him as he was when he first came wooing my sister, Patricia. Though a little bruised and soiled with pleasure, he was gallant, fine and vigorous, full of gaiety and truth…'

'…Of wit, charm and generosity,' proclaimed Alfie Schroeder, the famous columnist of the Billingsgate Press, over the coffin of the Provost, which had been moved from the Founder's Chantry to the centre of the aisle of the Choir; '…of charity, too, of tolerance and courtesy. Some of you may be wondering why Tom named me in his will to make the Oration before his burial. I will tell you.

'When Tom was a young man and I myself not so very old, we went into East Anglia together to unravel a mystery. I knew that he had the key to this, so I roused him from his bed in London, and persuaded him to travel with me; and together we came to Ely and thence to the little inns and hamlets in the Fens, to Luffham and then to Whereham…'

Well, yes, to Luffham and to Whereham, but all the rest rings false, thought Lord Luffham of Whereham, who recalled the whole affair clearly.* But if it is dubious as history, it may serve as epitaph.

'And together,' continued Alfie, 'we followed a trail that led to the Depths of a Flint Mine and thence to a Dancing Floor in a Sacred (or Diabolic) Wood, and finally to a crooked oratory in a crumbling church by a sedgebound lake…'

What piffle, thought Luffham of Whereham. They went to the vestry of the church, in excellent repair, that stood by a duck pond in the main street of the village.

'…And there read in a cobwebbed volume of parchment…'

The Parish Register, thought Luffham.

'…of the deep shame, or so it seemed at first, of a person in high places.'

Videlicet, thought Luffham, of me.

* See *The Rich Pay Later*, by Simon Raven (*Anthony Blond Ltd; 1964*).

'During that strange search,' Alfie went on, 'Tom Llewyllyn evinced all the learning, intellect and personal charisma – '

– OUCH –

' – that subsequently made him a man of esteem and distinction among both the gentles and the people. He also developed a new quality: humility. I like to think that it was I that taught him to be humble, and that he realized this, and that this is the reason why I am speaking to you, at his command, today.'

Alfie looked at the polite but quizzical audience that was ranged on either side of him, along the Choir. He looked down again, at his notes. He crumpled them into his pocket.

'Sweet Jesus Christ,' said Alfie. 'Tom Llewyllyn was a foul-mouthed, bilking, whoring piss-artist, dirty and smelly with it, and I just loved his fucking guts.'

With these words Sir Thomas Llewyllyn, Knt, D. Litt. and Litt. D., was introduced to the long home which he would thenceforth share with the monstrous cadaver of his grandson, in the Crypt of the College of which he had been Provost.

'*Kyrie, eleison*';
'*Christe, eleison*';
'*Kyrie, eleison.*'

After the coffin had been lowered into the Crypt, the Quiristers and the Congregation dispersed. Only the Fellows remained, seated in their stalls. As Len had foretold, since there were still several days to run before Term (let alone Full Term) would begin, and since he himself had not been officious in seeking out those absent, there were no Fellows present save friends, or at least more or less amical connections, of the dead Provost. The Senior among these, the Honourable Grantchester FitzMargrave Pough, Companion of Honour, now saw the last of the public out of the South Door, refused Len's request that he might stay and witness the proceedings ('The Secretary of the Provost, sir, is merely an upper servant, sir, and by no means to be admitted to the privilege of a Fellow'), locked the South Door on the inside, placed the key in a brass-bound chest, locked this with another key which he threw into the Font, limped impressively up the Nave, through the screen-arch, under the organ and into the Choir or Quire, and thus pronounced:

'By the Grace of God and our blessed and beloved Founder, I, Grantchester FitzMargrave Pough, Senior Fellow of this College, am at present paramount within it, the Provost being dead and the Vice-Provost beyond the sea and beyond recall.

'Normally, it would be my duty to instruct you that the Election of a New Provost must not be carried out until the return of our absent brethren and the coming of Full Term. However, since a grave crisis has arisen within our walls, I am required by Statute to proceed with the Election, however few of us may be present, forthwith, in order that the College may have authoritative and immediate guidance amid the perils that loom so near.'

What perils? thought Carmilla in her stall. This, of course, is some ruse of Len's, but what possible 'crisis' or 'peril' can he have fabricated?

'I refer,' said the Senior Fellow, 'to the grave matter of Miss Cora Corrington, Fellow of this College, niece of the late Miss Mona Corrington★, quondam Fellow of this College.'

Well, what about her? thought Carmilla. The Aunt had been a ripe old raving red, and rather sporty with it. Poor Cora, elected a Fellow about a year ago on the strength of research into the breeding habits of the Egyptian Moose-Beetle (*Bufo Aegyptianus*), was a dreary, mousy, plain little body, who spent her days in her laboratory and her nights in her chambers (dining off some scanty dish which she would order from the Kitchens), and had yet to address three words to anybody on

★ See *Places Where They Sing*, by Simon Raven (*Anthony Blond Ltd; 1970*).

any topic. What could poor Cora possibly have done to create a crisis?

But it now appeared, as Grantchester FitzMargrave Pough rumbled with relish through his tale, that many friends and followers of the rumbustious Aunt had adopted Cora, because of her name and blood, as the Figure Head of a Society devoted to promulgating and indeed implementing the doctrines of Mona and her lifelong associate and lover, Lord Beyfust★ (also dead). These sectaries were shortly to mount a ferocious demonstration it was alleged, using Cora's chambers in Lancaster as their base, against the present 'ethnic ratio' of the College, in which there were only fifteen negroes, ten brown jobs and three yellow, as against 415 whites. The cry was for 'racial equality', which in this instance apparently required black, brown, yellow and white to have one quarter each of the places available, and the same ratio to be set up in the Body of Fellows and the Members of the College Council as soon as possible. The Provost, so it was demanded by the Corrington-Beyfus Compassion Caucus (COBCOC for short) must be a mongrel comprising all four colours, if such could be found, or at the very least a half-caste.

'It is known,' said the Senior Fellow, 'that our respected colleague, Miss Cora Corrington, has been bullied and browbeaten, utterly against her will, into becoming titular head of the Caucus, changing her style from "Miss" to "M/S", and agreeing that her rooms should be used for the purpose of mounting the demonstration, and agreeing, furthermore, to provide refreshment for bibers of alcohol and carnivores. As one who has been a total abstainer and strict vegetarian since his early youth, I must deplore, nay condemn, the nature of the proposed refection, but that is by the way. The short truth is that a number of viragoes and male hooligans are about to rampage

★ See *Places Where They Sing*, by Simon Raven (*Anthony Blond Ltd; 1970*).

round this Holy College, demanding, with diabolic noise and violence, and for all I know with weapons, even firearms, that we change our entire constitution to suit their brand of fanatical bigotry.

'Plainly, this is not to be borne and must be stopped: equally plainly, strong leadership is instantly essential to stop it. We shall therefore elect a new Provost this very day, in absolute accordance with the Statute DCLXVI, 6, f, vi, *De Moribus Mutandis in Rebus Rabidis*, dated September 17, 1557, last invoked in August of 1914.'

Clever, thought Carmilla. There *was* a gang that was trying to use the reluctant Cora for her name and dead connections. There *had* been a strong rumour that they were planning a 'protest march' through the College, for the purpose of which they would slip in one by one, unnoticed and therefore unrepelled, gather in Cora's set at the South End of Sitwell's, and issue out screaming abuse and waving offensive banners and lewd images. So Len had blown the thing up, hinted at the use of lethal weapons, and hey-presto (thought Carmilla) we have a full-scale revolution on our hands and therefore the right to elect, although we represent only a tiny minority of the College Council, a Provost of our choice.

'There are two candidates,' continued Pough: 'Mr Ivor Winstanley and Sir Jacquiz Helmutt. You know them both too well to need further introduction from me. You will now signify your preference in the accustomed manner.'

He himself, as senior man present, creaked down from his stall, up the Choir towards the Altar, and so to the edge of the great rectangle of darkness through which Sir Tom's coffin had descended. Opposite him and upright, at the far end of the rectangle and only a few paces from the altar steps, was the slab of marble that had been raised from the floor that Llewyllyn might be lowered through it. Grantchester Pough bowed, walked along the left (Northern) side of the rectangle, peering down into it as though seeking guidance or approval from those

29

below (Christ, let him not fall in, thought Balbo Blakeney, for that would fuck the proceedings right up), moved round to stand by the East face of the slab and worked a screw of paper into one of a large phalanx of holes bored into the marble.

'*Praebui meam voluntatem,*' proclaimed Pough; *fiat voluntas mea. In nomine Dei and beati Henrici.* I have declared my will; my will be done. In the name of God and the blessèd Henry.'

Balbo Blakeney now came out to declare his will. As he edged along the dark rectangle, looking down for guidance, Carmilla saw him start and nearly fall, then recover himself, smile down into the pit with great sweetness, and raise a hand, either in greeting or farewell. Sentimental old thing, she thought, as her eyes pricked.

'*Praebui meam voluntatem,*' called Balbo, as he posted his screw of paper; '*fiat voluntas mea.*'

Of course, reflected Carmilla; only the senior man present was allowed to invoke God and the blessèd Henry after making his vote.

Balbo returned to his stall. The remaining seven Fellows followed him one by one. Last but two went Carmilla; last of all the wretched Cora Corrington. As Junior Fellow present she had her own special invocation.

'…*Fiat voluntas mea,*' she intoned. '*In nomine cupidine Mariae Magdalenae in corpus Domini Nostri.* In the name of Mary Magdalen's desire for the body of Our Lord. Amen.'

This last bit had been put in, so Carmilla had been told by Len, as a fitting acknowledgement of the frailty of the flesh even amidst the purest aspiration of the spirit – as an admission that even the Fellows of Lancaster when electing a new Provost might err from petty human partialities.

Grantchester Pough now prowled infirmly up the Choir once more, to stand before the East face of the slab and collect the votes from the special cavities. Having done so he chanted (in remarkably good voice for a near-centenarian), 'O Man of Mightiness, let the Worm inherit thee,' and pushed the slab, which revolved on its hinge and sank to rest with a low boom.

Pough then retired to the Founder's Chantry to count the votes. The rest gathered by the Font. Five minutes later Pough came to them and said, 'I give you tidings of great joy. We have a Provost, duly and unanimously elected: Sir Jacquiz Helmutt. Approach the Font, Sir Knight.'

As Helmutt did so, all present scooped up water with their cupped hands and cast it into Sir Jacquiz' face. Ivor Winstanley did this with unseemly and spiteful vigour, for although he had not hoped or indeed wished to be elected, he should, he knew, have had at least one vote, that of his rival; for custom constrained opponents to vote for each other. Clearly Sir Jacquiz had neglected this courteous practice, and this, after all the years they had spent playing Royal Tennis together, was vexing and ungenerous. But Helmutt did not appear to notice his old friend's little spurt of viciousness. He bowed gracefully in the Tudor manner as Pough, presenting him with the key of the chest (fished out of the Font) that held the key to the South Door, resonantly proclaimed:

'The Provost, having been duly and fully baptized, let no man seek to oust him against his will now or hereafter, while yet he shall breathe, *in nomine Dei et beati Henrici*. Amen.'

'Amen,' responded all present with a great shout of triumph; '*In nomine Dei et beati Henrici*. Amen. Amen. Amen.'

'I suppose,' said Carmilla to Balbo in the Withdrawing-Room of the Provost's Lodging, 'that we *are* the last College to elect a Provost for life, should he wish to stay that long? "Let no man seek to oust him against his will while yet he shall breathe." '

They were now at the old Provost's *Vale* and the new Provost's *Ave*, the ceremonies being by custom combined and calling for the most luxurious food and drink to be had in the Kingdom of this World. While Balbo was helping Carmilla to vodka and fresh Beluga, and explaining that Lancaster was indeed the only College to elect a Provost for life and that this was because a Provost, being the Avatar of the Founder, could not conceivably be removed unless he asked to be, Marigold Helmutt came up, rather breathless.

'Congratulations on Jacquiz' elevation,' said Balbo.

Marigold did not appear to have heard him.

'Have you seen my twins?' she said. 'They seem to have vanished. They came to the South Door with me when we were all pushed out so you lot could have your election, and when I looked around a few minutes later, they'd just vanished.'

'I saw 'em,' said Balbo. 'During the election. They were in the Crypt.'

'*Crypt?*'

'Under the opening where they wind the slab back for the coffin to be lowered. As I went past toward the Altar to post my vote, I looked down and there were your twins...standing on a coffin right beneath. It must have been Tom's. They were looking straight up at me. Smiling.'

'They never smiled at anyone in their whole lives.'

'They smiled at me. I gave a kind of salute with my arm, and they waved back, as if saying goodbye. If you ask me, they're off.'

'Oh,' said Marigold. 'I hope they know I love them. Why,' she said, in a fierce pet of jealousy, 'should they make such a thing of saying goodbye to you?'

'I was there...when it all happened.* Remember?'

'So was I. And I'm their mother.'

'I don't think that counts for much, not with them. Nor do I count for much, Marigold. It's just that they needed someone to know that they were going, someone to pass on the word,

* See *The Roses of Picardie*, by Simon Raven (*House of Stratus; 2001*).

and I was convenient. So they made the conventional human signs to me.'

'Why couldn't they just tell us all?'

'You know they hate talking,' said Balbo. 'When did they last talk...to anybody?'

'Come to think of it, I'm not sure they ever have. They make their wants known somehow, and you feel as if they were talking,' said Marigold, 'but really they're simply pointing at things or making gestures. Last time they wanted to go abroad – to Egypt it was – they just produced a brochure and showed me a photograph and then stood there looking at me. Ah well,' said Marigold, who had her own rather peculiar notions about the whole business, 'I suppose we'll just have to leave it at that. But there will be a gap.'

'But where can they have gone?' said Carmilla. 'If they didn't get out of the Crypt before that slab went down, where could they possibly have gone?'

'Don't worry yourself about them,' said Marigold, who was a sensible woman and had long foreseen something of the kind (though there would still, as she said, be a gap): 'they should know their way about...where they are. Shouldn't they, Balbo?'

Balbo and Marigold exchanged a fond look. Carmilla, left out of it, sighed and turned her head, till she could see Jeremy Morrison, Fielding Gray and Marius Stern, who were talking very closely away in one corner.

Male conclave, keep out, Carmilla thought: no one wants Carmilla just now. But she was wrong. Rosie Stern and Tessa Malcolm were standing hand in hand (the evening and the morning, Carmilla thought) at Carmilla's elbow.

'Come with us into the garden,' Rosie said. 'It may be the last time we shall see it, now Uncle Tom is dead.'

'Provost Helmutt will invite us,' said Carmilla.

'You perhaps. I do not know the Provost Helmutt,' Rosie said. 'Please come into the garden. We have something to ask you, Tessa and I.'

Since Tessa was loved by her sister, Theodosia, and Rosie was the sister of her own Marius, Carmilla went with them, though she had never liked the garden of the Provost's Lodging. Provost Llewyllyn had once said that the nymphs of the College Elm Trees (or their ghosts) had taken refuge there and still lingered with malignant purpose. Carmilla half believed this: she believed, at any rate, that the Provost believed it, and did not walk, for choice, in the garden. However, at Rosie's behest and Tessa's, she went there now.

As Carmilla and the two girls passed Jeremy and Co. in the corner, Carmilla caught Jeremy's words,

'But what shall we do about Mrs Malcolm?'

They're discussing their getaway, Carmilla thought; what a day for departures.

When they were in the garden, Tessa said:

'They were talking of Mrs Malcolm. My Auntie Maisie. They seemed to think she was going to be upset.'

'Jeremy and Fielding are going away on a journey,' said Carmilla. 'They're worried that your Aunt will be lonely.'

Tessa's face became very thoughtful.

'My fault as much as anyone's,' she said in her husky little voice, 'being away so long with your sister. But there is something else we have to discuss just now.'

'Marius,' said Rosie: 'we thought you might be able to help us about him.'

And so the three of them began, rather tentatively, to discuss the matter of Marius…

…Who, meanwhile, was listening to Jeremy and Fielding, while they arranged their journey to Ithaca.

'I wish I was coming with you to Ithaca,' Marius said. 'I know I can't come on your voyage, but just as far as Ithaca…to see you off? You still owe me a journey, as that one to the East never happened.'

'You know very well what happened about *that*,' said Jeremy: 'I was in the slammer in Oz.'

'You still owe me a journey.'

'Not this one,' said Jeremy; 'you've got your O Levels to think about.' And to Fielding: 'You still haven't said what you're going to do about Maisie Malcolm.'

'I'm going back to Broughton tomorrow morning,' Fielding said; 'and there I shall tell her that September is nearly done and that it is time to go back to business in London. That hotel may run pretty well without her, but it's time she went back for a good look at it.'

'Will she like that?' Marius said.

'She'll be damned ungrateful if she doesn't. I've been down there with her for weeks.'

'She won't like your going off again with me,' Jeremy said.

'She'll be lonely next hols,' said Marius. 'Rosie will be in France with our mama, and I shall be with Auntie Flo in Somerset, and Tessa will be with Theodosia Canteloupe. What will Mrs Malcolm do at Christmas? None of us, you see, can invite her to where we shall be. She simply wouldn't fit.'

There was an uneasy silence.

'Nothing to be done about that,' said Fielding at last, shiftily but at the same time finally. 'So: Jeremy: you're for London tomorrow and all those interviews and so on which they're setting up to puff your Byronic voyage…and the book you're going to write at the end of it…'

'…The book which you are going to write with me.'

'We'll see about that when the time comes. But I'm your man for the voyage, as you know. Get us flights to Athens and berths on a boat to Ithaca, would you? Leaving as soon as you reckon your interviews will be done. First Class, of course, as the old firm will be paying.'

'Yes,' said Marius: 'Salinger, Stern & Detterling will be paying. Your faithful publishers, of whom I am one of the larger shareholders, do not forget, though not as large as Carmilla Salinger or my Lady Canteloupe. I suppose we can run to First Class in your case: if not, Mr Ashley Dexterside will no doubt advise us.'

'Who's Mr Ashley Dexterside?' Jeremy enquired.

'The General Manager. With the firm from the very beginning, when it was just Salinger & Holbrook in three grotty rooms in Chancery Lane. A generation before it merged with Stern & Detterling.'

'Who was Holbrook?' said Jeremy. 'I've often wondered.'

'Holbrook was very bad news,' said Marius. 'Luckily he disappeared very early – long before Carmilla and Theodosia were adopted by poor Donald Salinger.'

'How do you know so much?' said Fielding.

'I went there one day to meet everybody,' said Marius. "Always let them get a look at you," my old Dad used to say. "Make sure they know your face – and you know theirs and can put a name to them." So one day I went there, and was shown round by Mr Dexterside – who fancied me like fury in a respectful sort of way. He told me lots of very interesting things – about the slut poor Donald married and how cruel she was to Carmilla and Thea when they were little girls; about her hideous death in a haunted wood on the Kent coast – oddly enough, a place I'd once been to with my mother and father – '

' – Did you see the ghost?' Fielding asked –

' – And all about the ghastly Holbrook,' said Marius, who did not appear to have heard Fielding's question, 'how he got in with crooks and had to disappear forever.'

'Not quite forever,' Fielding said. 'Tom and I once found him in a marsh near Venice. Not a happy man.'

'Salinger & Holbrook,' said Marius, 'was not a very happy firm, or not when it started. What with Donald Salinger's slut and his partner Holbrook's criminals…And another thing Mr Dexterside told me: apparently one of the first secretaries the firm ever had was an old witch called Miss Beatty, who was beheaded by a sex maniac in 1956. "Loathsome hag," said Mr Dexterside; "beheading was much too good for her." '

In the garden, Carmilla Salinger was still discussing Marius with the two girls.

'It was to talk with you that we really came,' said Rosie Stern, after several commonplace exchanges about Marius' work (O Levels this coming December), cricket (Under Sixteen Cap last quarter), fives and racquets (good prospects this quarter), and so forth. 'Officially,' said Rosie, 'I'm here to represent Mummy and Tessa's here to keep me company, but in fact Marius could perfectly well have represented our mother without my being here at all. And so they said at School. But I insisted on coming, and begged them to let Tessa come with me – all so that we could talk with you…ask you questions, one in particular.'

'Ask.'

'Tessa has told me, in strict confidence, that Marius is the father of the child which your sister is bearing.'

They all looked in through the open door at gibbous Theodosia, who was standing in the Withdrawing-Room, under a huge candelabrum which writhed out from the wall, talking with Canteloupe and Jacquiz Helmutt.

'Tessa has also told me about her and Lady Canteloupe,' Rosie said in the garden.

'Have you any objection to prefer on either count?' said Carmilla.

'No. I simply want to ask you some questions, as I said.'

'Then I repeat: ask.'

Rosie stroked her raven hair from crown to shoulder.

'First,' said Rosie: 'they say that there have been tests and that Lady Canteloupe's child will be a girl?'

'True,' said Carmilla.

'Next: Tessa says that Canteloupe will require his wife to try again, with Marius, for a boy?'

'Perhaps,' said Carmilla.

'Next,' said Rosie. 'I know that Marius is very much under the influence of Mr Raisley Conyngham, at our School. How much has he to do with all this over Marius and Lady Canteloupe?'

'Nothing,' said Carmilla. 'Raisley Conyngham knows what is going on between them, he condones and approves it, but none of it has been arranged by him. The decisions are those of Canteloupe and Theodosia: Canteloupe has wished for children and Theodosia has consented to have them fathered on her by a man of her choice – Marius Stern. As for Mr Conyngham, we think that he has plans of his own for Marius.'

'What plans?'

'We do not know.'

'Plans…that will wound Marius…or even destroy him?'

'We believe that Mr Conyngham wishes to possess Marius, mind, soul and spirit, and will try to involve him in processes of thought and action that will finally bind him utterly to Mr Conyngham's will. We believe that Mr Conyngham has been trying to do this for some time, but that so far, by God's grace, he has failed.'

'Do you really mean, "By God's grace"?' asked Tessa, bending to pick a small blue flower from a border.

'A polite and dishonest fashion of speech,' said Carmilla. 'I mean, by sheer luck. Whatever result God may wish for this contest – assuming, that is, that He has any interest in it at all – He will help nobody. He means that we should help ourselves.'

'Then last of all,' said Rosie: 'can you limit or contain Marius and his activities in such a way that he goes no further than doing those things in which he is engaged with your sister now – things which, you say, Mr Conyngham merely condones or approves, but are not directly willed or suggested by him? Can you ensure that Marius is not so far enticed by Mr Conyngham as to be possessed by him, to do his whole bidding, and become a creature of his will?'

'I don't quite understand,' said Carmilla, 'why you seem to be charging me with this office. I wish Marius very well, but I have many other things to attend to, including a book of which I have hopes. I think we should all ask ourselves whether Marius' salvation may not depend on Marius' own efforts.'

'After all,' said Tessa, 'it should not be so difficult for Marius to save himself. When Mr Conyngham tried to possess me in this way, I just walked out.'

'You have a healthy soul,' said Rosie, tugging at her raven hair; 'Marius does not.'

'Rather an important point,' said Carmilla. She took Rosie's hand and detached it from her hair, then smiled at Tessa. 'But let me leave you both with this thought. I have good reason to suppose,' she said, referring to her new relation with Marius but not yet wishing to own it overtly, important as it might be to the end which they all had in view, 'that Mr Raisley Conyngham will be, from now on, a diminishing influence on the attitudes and actions of Marius Stern.'

Raisley Conyngham and Milo Hedley were sitting on a bench on the boundary of the School Cricket Green, which was now, since September was far advanced, peopled only by the ghosts of vanished summers.

'On reflection,' said Raisley, 'I think you were right to let Marius stay over in Lancaster till the Provost's Burial.'

'Thank you, sir.'

'But the Burial is today. At this very moment, in fact. Marius will be back here tomorrow. Let us consider.'

'I must be gone tomorrow, sir. I must see to the furnishing of my rooms in Trinity.'

'You will not be needed, *vis-à-vis* Marius, tomorrow. No action is required of either of us for some little while. *But we must consider.* Now hear me, Milo. Last August we nearly had our way. We so nearly had Marius to do our absolute will. But at the last minute we were frustrated. Just as Marius was about to kill little Lord Sarum (for kill him he would have) there was unlooked-for interference. And so, although Sarum did indeed die, he did not die by Marius' hand and by our command. Therefore Marius remains guiltless and my plan, to make him responsible, by my devising, for the greatest crime of all, has failed.'

'But surely, sir, Marius was so deeply involved, so thoroughly determined to see the thing through, that morally he did kill Sarum – though not with his own hands. And certainly you can have the pleasure of knowing that Sarum's death came about by just that sort of discreet progression that you would have wished…a progression of unremarkable events of which one preceded another in an absolutely ordinary and day-to-day manner, humdrum cause preceding commonplace effect in a series so dull, so utterly devoid of note, that even though the final consequence was violent death nobody was seriously exposed to public blame or attention at any stage.'

'Yes, yes, Milo. As an *operation* the killing of Sarum was a great success. And thereby we have obliged both Canteloupe and Glastonbury, to the extent that whether they like it or not they are now in very deep collusion with us – all of which may prove very useful indeed. But nevertheless, Milo, the thing did not end as I would have wished. Marius had no speck of blood on him, and as you know I wished him to be committed to us –'

' – He is committed to us –'

' – I wished him to be totally and perpetually committed to us, Milo, by the actual shedding of bright blood brought about by our will and direction. Mind you, what *did* occur was far more easily explained to the police and far more quickly forgotten by the world – and I was entirely happy that Marius should have the benefit of those factors. But the plain truth is that we did not bring Marius to the right true end to which we seek to bring him, and now we must think again.'

'It is unlikely that we shall have the opportunity to stage another killing.'

'Very unlikely, and just as well. Killings, Milo, are rather hard on the nerves. But I think I know what we can line up for Marius. What about…treachery, Milo, or betrayal, of a kind *not* involving bother with the police: personal betrayal.'

Despite long acquaintance with Raisley Conyngham and his ways, Milo shivered.

'You would make of him a Judas?' he said.

'It is one thought that I have had. You may have others. Meanwhile, think carefully, Milo, while you are furnishing your delightful rooms in Trinity, what kind of treachery, and to whom, would bring in any sort of benefit for you or me…or one of our associates. For if something or other useful can be achieved or gained, or if somebody or other can be usefully served by the new sequence of cause and effect in which we shall later insert Marius, then so much the better. Waste not, want not, as they say.'

After a while Canteloupe found a curved and gilded Hepplewhite throne for pregnant Theodosia to sit on, and they both held court at one end of the Provost's Withdrawing-Room. Major Fielding Gray and the Honble Mr Jeremy Morrison paid their respects, as did Piero Caspar, of Black-fork Fen in the County of Cambridge, Esquire, who had first met Canteloupe in very different circumstances.

'So you are to be a Fellow here?' said Canteloupe.

'*Si*, milor,' grinned Piero.

'And you've inherited the bulk of that old rotter Tunne's money and estates.'

'*Si, si*, milor.'

'So. May God or the Devil give you joy of your good fortune, Piero.'

'I pray that one of them may, milor. And yet I am so sad for good Sir Thomas.'

And Piero retired, tears dripping down his face, as he remembered the days in Venice with Canteloupe and Miss Baby and plain Tom Llewyllyn (as he was then) and dead Daniel Mond.★ Tom had loathed him then, he knew, but surely, later, had come love?

Then Balbo Blakeney came to make his bow to the Canteloupes, and Lord Luffham of Whereham, and even the new Provost himself; Greco Barraclough and Nicos Pandouros, Alfie Schroeder, the popular columnist of the Billingsgate Press, Ivor Winstanley the Latinist and Lord Burgo Gaviston the Grecian. For a rich and mighty Prince was the Marquess Canteloupe upon this earth, and the people thereof made obeisance before him, even when he was on another's ground, that of the blessèd King Henry VI. Last to come were Carmilla, her ladyship's sister, and Marius, the father of the child her ladyship was bearing. Marius was nervous, as he had last parted with Lady Canteloupe, not indeed in anger, but in doubt. Today, however, Theodosia smiled at him and kissed him full on the lips.

'Go and talk to your sister, Rosie,' she said: 'Canty and I want a word with Carmilla.'

'But I see Rosie every day at School, and I hardly ever see you, Thea – '

' – Stop grizzling and go and talk to Rosie and Tessa,' Carmilla said; and Marius went.

'Good,' said Theodosia.

'Yes,' agreed Carmilla. ' "I say to one 'Go' and he goeth".'

'So we see. But will your influence prevail to keep him clear of Conyngham?'

'I hope so,' Carmilla said.

★ See *The Survivors*, by Simon Raven (*Blond & Briggs; 1976*).

Carmilla stood in front of her twin and slightly to the right of her. Just behind Lady Canteloupe and on her left Lord Canteloupe courteously and casually attended on the women and their conversation.

'But you will be here in Cambridge,' Theodosia said to Carmilla. 'Conyngham, down in Farncombe, will be sitting right over Marius, teaching him to make his pretty verses. Why don't they send that man away from that School?'

'Because he is respectable and has a long and brilliant record as a tutor,' said Carmilla. 'Nothing whatever can be proved against him on any count. True, he is rich: but even these days a man cannot be dismissed from his post for that.'

'So he remains at his post – to hover with his black wings over Marius.'

'I have been talking with Rosie and Tessa,' Carmilla said. 'They will watch Marius at School. I shall go there often. For his exeats and so on he will come here, or go to Tessa's Auntie Maisie at Buttock's Hotel, or to our friend Florence at Sandy Lodge.'

'To his mother in France, perhaps, when Rosie goes?'

'His mother does not want him there. When he was a little boy,' said Carmilla, 'she treated him as a lover. Now he is almost a man she feels this would be inappropriate; in any case they quarrel about politics and money.'

'But the important thing is,' said Thea, 'that you reckon, between you, to keep him safe.'

'Oh yes,' said Carmilla: 'we surely have him now.'

That's all you know, thought Canteloupe, remembering the events of the previous August and thinking of the many things that his old friend, Giles Glastonbury, his old comrade in arms and conspiracy, had told him about Raisley Conyngham. Just because Marius had got a temporary lech for Carmilla and vice versa (for I suppose that's what's up, thought Canteloupe), she thinks, like all women in that situation, that she's got him for good. And she thinks, in her complacency, that when she's not there those two little girls can serve as her agents and his angels. Raisley Conyngham, thought Canteloupe, has only to raise one little finger to Marius and Marius will come running like Achilles, sweeping this whole pack of chattering women to the floor.

Sir Jacquiz Helmutt, who was sitting in the downstairs loo in the Provost's Lodging munching cold partridge stuffed with chestnuts and taking a well-earned rest from adulation, was annoyed at a banging on the door.

'Come on, Jake,' said Marigold: 'I know you're in there.'

'And why should I not be?'

'I've got news.'

'I can hear you very well through this door.'

'So can too many people this side of it.'

'All right. Come in.' Jacquiz unlocked the door, whisked her inside, locked it again, and resumed his seat.

'Why have you taken down your trousers,' she said, 'when you're only in here to eat a partridge?'

'I'm here for the other thing too.'

'Not very kosher of you.'

'Tell me this news that is so urgent.'

'The twins have gone,' said Marigold. 'Last seen by Balbo, down in the Crypt. He says they smiled and waved.'

'We always knew they would go, Marigold. Do not be sad. But I could wish they had smiled and waved to you and me before they went.'

'Balbo thinks the smile and the wave were for all of us. He just happened to be in the right place at the right time.'

This was bending the truth a bit, but she did not want to mar his day of triumph more than she need.

'Where have they gone, think you?'

'Back where they came from,' Marigold said. 'Where they were...begotten. And where they lived...in the time before that. If you remember, Jaky, it was always to Greece, Turkey,

Israel or Egypt that they wished us to take them. They must have been finding out whether they would be welcome back.'

'And they found they would be?' said Jacquiz, getting off the loo and dropping the remains of his partridge into it. 'And so they have returned?'

'Yes; so I think. As time goes on, Jacquiz, their absence will be noticed and reported, and the police will want to know where they have gone. They will not believe what we have to tell them.'

Jacquiz began, thoughtfully and carefully, to prepare himself to return to the party. 'Yes,' he agreed. 'We need to prepare and issue an explanation before anyone starts asking for one. Would Dr La Soeur put them on his books? As inmates of his Nursing Home? He could arrange substitutions if anyone came to enquire there.'

'Dr La Soeur has retired at last,' Marigold said.

'His Nursing Home is still running.'

'He no longer takes risks.'

'Then I have it. I have an acquaintance, an American secret agent – Earle Restarick, he is called. He was very much involved with poor Daniel in Germany nearly thirty years ago. A horrible affair...* and after Daniel's unexpected recovery from it, Restarick came to see me, as Daniel's most Jewish friend, to find out certain things about him – and to make sure he would be harmless from now on. I reassured him and we have been in touch ever since. Occasional services on either side, you understand: I give him information about big people in my world, and he arranges permission for excavations or exports with awkward Eastern officials. He is now in Constantinople, Marigold. I shall tell him what has happened: I shall arrange for him to write to us, once a month, giving an account of the

---

* See *The Sabre Squadron*, by Simon Raven (*Blond & Briggs Ltd; 1971*).

twins, as if they had gone for special education there, under his supervision.'

'It looks as if that's what they have done. Not under his supervision, of course,' Marigold said, 'but in his kind of area. Ask him to keep an eye open. One day,' said Marigold with a quick sob, 'they might actually turn up.'

Rosie and Tessa went into Lancaster Chapel.

'I must see those windows again before we go,' said Tessa. The two girls would spend the night in a College Guest Room, and then return to School with Marius the next day.

'The light will be better tomorrow morning,' Rosie said.

'There will be more people around tomorrow morning,' said Tessa. 'And perhaps Marius will be impatient and make us hurry.'

The Choir was chanting evensong in the Chancel. They peeped through the arch of the Rood Screen. A ray from a candle made a split second halo of red gold round Tessa's head. Rosie trembled.

'It would be bad manners, to go through to the Choir,' said Rosie, pulling herself together, 'in the middle of this lovely singing. Besides, I'm not sure I wish to go up there again after seeing that horrible yawning pit this afternoon.'

'The slab that covers it will have been lowered by now,' Tessa said.

'Even so...Let's just sit here and listen to the Choir. We can hear perfectly well through the screen.'

After a while, Rosie went on: 'You didn't speak to Lady Canteloupe at the party?'

'The occasion was not right,' said Tessa. 'She had her duties and I had mine. I shall see her during our first exeat, and then there will be nobody, for most of the time, but us.'

'Do you think her sister, Carmilla, is right about Marius? That from now on he will be less closely involved with Mr Conyngham?'

'I dare say,' said Tessa: 'we shall see.'

'We have promised to watch. If she is not right, we can soon tell her.'

'But what would she do about it?' Tessa said.

'She is very rich.'

'So are you and Marius.'

'Not as rich as her,' said Rosie. 'She could arrange...for almost anything.'

'Special arrangements,' said Tessa, 'are not what we want for Marius. He thinks himself much too special already. We simply want things to go on as usual. "Keep the even tenor of their way",' quoted Tessa, remembering Grey's *Elegy*, one of last year's Set Poems.

'That is hoping for rather a lot,' said Rosie, 'in this sort of a circus.'

Before he left the Provost's Lodging, Lord Luffham of Whereham found time for a word with his son, Jeremy Morrison.

'I've had seats put up in your memory,' he said: 'at School, and in the garden of this Lodging, and in lots of other places.'

'You mean...as if I were dead, sir?'

'Something of the kind. It's not that business of your going to gaol that I mind – any of us might have landed in there at some stage – it was that "Back to the Earth Mother" rubbish. I cannot stand for popular hysteria of that kind, still less for those that get it up.'

'It was only a joke, father. I wanted to see how far it would go, how long I could get away with it.'

'That, I agree, might have been interesting; but of course the thing collapsed when you were caught offering your bottom around. How much longer do you think your movement would have survived had it not been for that little accident?'

'It was going pretty strong. But I was getting bored.'

'Yes, that always was your trouble,' said Luffham of Whereham: 'no staying power. And so now, they tell me, you're off in a boat with Fielding Gray. Looking for the Hesperides, or some such thing. What's to become of the estate?'

'Looking for the Isles of the Blessèd or Blest, sir. There is a difference, you know. The Hesperides have golden apples, while the Isles of the Blest are inhabited by the upper-class dead. Jason and that lot.'

'We were talking of an estate which belongs to the upperclass living. What's to become of Luffham? It's yours now, as you very well know.'

'Oh yes indeed, sir. I went down there the other day. They're touchingly loyal, all of them, and attribute my little bit of bother to a "breakdown". So they rather expect me to take a long holiday now, father. The agent will cope very well.'

'Better than you, as I've always told you. Ah, Fielding,' said Luffham, as Fielding Gray approached, 'I hear you and Jeremy are off boating in the Mediterranean. Following the route of Odysseus – something of that kind?'

'Not quite, Peter. Following the route Odysseus *would* have taken when he set out from Ithaca the second time.'

'Rather hypothetical?'

'We know, at least, that he went West.'

'Who says so? I've already put my foot in it with Master Pedant here by confusing the Hesperides with the Isles of the Blest, and of course I was never, as you know, a classical man, but I thought the whole point of the story was that Odysseus longed to get back to his wife,' said Luffham, thinking with a bitter pang of his own dead Helen, 'and stay with her forever.'

'There are other versions,' Fielding said. 'A Greek poet called Kazantzakis – '

' – An appalling and grossly conceited bore,' said Luffham, 'who's only been dead a few years. Even I know that. Why should we believe Kazantzakis? Didn't he write some silly lies about Jesus Christ? Said He had it off with the Magdalen when they were both eleven – something like that?'

'He is not the only man,' said Fielding, 'to have written silly lies about someone called Jesus Christ. There are the four Evangelists, for a start, to say nothing of Saint Paul – '

' – I'm not blaming him for getting Christ wrong,' said Luffham; 'I just see no reason to suppose that he got Odysseus right.'

'Tennyson supports the idea – that Odysseus sailed away a second time. To the West.'

'And what would Tennyson know about it? Drunk the whole time.'

'That was his descendant, Peter, the one that captained England at cricket,' said Fielding.

'There *is* quite an amusing legend, father,' Jeremy put in, 'that Odysseus was told by an oracle to sail West until he came to a shore, then walk inland carrying an oar over his shoulder until someone stopped him and asked him for the loan of his winnowing fan. There he was meant to settle. Or dig his grave. I forget which.'

'If you sailed due West from Ithaca,' his father said, 'you would strike the Eastern coast of Cephalonia after a very few miles. Are you going to get out and carry an oar inland there? You'd hit the sea again in ten minutes.'

'I do not propose to carry an oar anywhere at all,' said Jeremy patiently. 'I was simply citing a legend to indicate the persistence, albeit in very various forms, of the tradition. Fielding and I, father, are charged to sail West until we come to a place which I shall know, in my heart, means the same to me as the Isles of the Blest would have meant to Odysseus. As you aptly remark, there can be no question of sailing literally due West. Even where it is possible to do so over open sea, we are far too inexperienced mariners to attempt any such thing. And so, father, very broadly speaking, we shall follow the northern coastline of the Mediterranean, winding about a great deal but always proceeding, in the long run, towards the West, until one day…one day…'

'…You will arrive at the Isles of the Blest, about which, the advance publicity seems to be saying, you will write a book. No doubt Fielding can help you. He is a good hand at writing books, Fielding is. And if you don't find your islands or whatever, he will have no trouble inventing them.'

'But now will you wish me luck, father? I shall not see you again before I sail.'

'With all my heart. You too, Fielding.' Luffham shook Fielding by the hand in a sturdy fashion. Then he turned to his son, leaned forward and kissed him on the forehead, then touched him lightly on his fluffy fair hair.

' "But there," he said, "my blessing with thee." Go well, Jeremy.'

'Stay well, father,' Jeremy said.

When Fielding Gray arrived back in Broughton Staithe on the morning after the Provost's Burial, Maisie was sitting on her folding chair among the ruined gun-sites in the sand dunes, reading Samuel Richardson's *Clarissa*.

'Christ, that silly boring girl don't half go on about keeping herself proper,' Maisie said when Fielding had walked across the golf course to announce his return.

'Anyone would think that a popped hole was the pit of Hell. Does Lovelace have his wicked way with her before page two thousand?'

'You must read on and find out for yourself, my love. But I'm afraid the reading party is over here in Broughton. I've got to be off now…though I suppose you could stay if you wished.'

'No thank you, dear,' said Maisie, taking all this very quietly. 'We've had a very nice long time together down here, you and I, with three or four very jolly little expeditions down Remembrance Lane – '

' – Memory Lane – '

' – Remembrance Lane, dear, like Remembrance Sunday, for something that's long dead and gone and which takes a lot of puffing and blowing of trumpets to get it going again. But jolly it was, I'm not denying it, and I've read enough books here in these dunes to qualify for a doctorate of letters, and now the autumn's here and it's time I got myself back to London and spruced up my old hotel.'

'Right. Off this afternoon?'

'No point,' said Maisie, 'in hanging about. Where are you going? And how long for?'

'The Mediterranean. For an indefinite period. With Jeremy Morrison.'

Might as well tell her about Jeremy at once, he thought: she'll have to know soon anyway.

'That nasty great white turd? So they've let him out of that slammer in Oz?'

'Yes. He's going on an exploration, and he's going to need company. Although I deserted him in Australia – '

' – Couldn't do much else, could you, when the coppers had tooken him off?'

' – I could have stayed there. Stood by him. But although I didn't, he's asked me to go with him now, and go I must.'

'Where?' Maisie gathered her six or seven books into a plastic carrier. 'Where in the Mediterranean, I mean?'

'To Ithaca. Odysseus his Kingdom.'

'Odysseus?' said Maisie, rising creakily.

'Ulysses.'

'Hmm. I like Odysseus better, now you've told me.'

'Good. It's the proper Greek name.'

'What are you going to do in Ithaca?'

'Sail away from it. Westward ho.'

'Oh. Be back for Christmas, will you?'

'I don't know, Maisie.'

They began to walk across the ninth fairway of the golf course, Fielding carrying the folding chair, but not the bag of books, which Maisie insisted on clasping to her left breast as if it had been an infant at suck.

'Well, if you're not back at Christmas, don't ring up,' Maisie said.

'I doubt if I should be able to.'

'Able or not, don't ring up. There's nothing worse than being rung up when you're spending a lonely Christmas.'

As soon as he was back at School, Marius waited on Raisley Conyngham in his study in his chambers, where they were due to consider a piece of Greek Iambic Verse which Marius had written in translation of Othello's final speech.

'Good,' said Raisley Conyngham, holding the copy high in front of him and then plonking it down on his desk; 'too many tribrachs and anapaests. Otherwise good.'

'I thought, sir, that the mood of the speech demanded much variation of rhythm. Hence the tribrachs and the ana – '

' – Precisely.'

'But you've just said there are too many of them.'

'There were. I'm afraid few examiners would react to Othello's speech with your sensitivity. Whatever the nature of the English, they would be looking,' said Raisley, 'for standard Greek Iambics dominated by the Iamb. It is the examiners you have to satisfy, Marius, not your own aesthetic sense. More of this anon. How was Cambridge?'

'Agreeable, sir.'

'And how was Carmilla Salinger?'

'Why do you ask, sir?' said Marius, shifting his feet.

'A simple enquiry after the young lady's health. I imagined that in the circumstances – quite apart from the fact that you are a fellow shareholder in Salinger, Stern & Detterling – you would certainly see her and speak with her in the sad course of the obsequies and their aftermath. Since my routine enquiry has elicited an uneasy response, I assume something shameful took place.'

'Nothing shameful, sir.'

'Well then, what? Please do not forget, Marius, that you are under an oath of obedience.'

'I remember, sir. Holkam. During that storm.'

'Of course you remember. That storm. What do storms suggest to a well-read man? Dido and Aeneas copulating in a cave? Ah, I see you blink. Did you and Carmilla Salinger copulate in a cave?'

'Nothing so dramatic, sir. She started...by playing with me. She knew I was keen. And I played with her. Then it got more serious.'

'You mean she loves you?'

'At least she intends it should last. She has me...at heart.'

'And you have her at heart?'

'I enjoy her,' said Marius, 'and I am grateful to her. I should like to please her, and I should be sorry to give her pain.'

'And your oath? Your committal to Milo and myself?'

'Why should that conflict with my affection for Miss Salinger?'

'Why indeed?' said Raisley. 'Now then: Thomas Lovell Beddoes, an old boy of this School, once wrote a pretty lyric:

> "If there were dreams to sell,
> What would you buy?
> Some cost a passing bell,
> Some a light sigh..."

'You will find the full text in Iredale's edition of Beddoes in the School Library. Translate the entire poem, by next Friday noon, first into a copy of Latin Elegiacs that would satisfy the criteria of a pedantic examiner; next into a copy of Greek Elegiacs that would achieve the same; and thirdly, to satisfy your own poetic genius, into any Latin or Greek lyric metre, consulting only your own inclination and taste.'

'So,' said Isobel Stern to Jo-Jo Guiscard, as they walked with Jo-Jo's little daughter Oenone in the cloister of the Cathedral of St-Bertrand-de-Comminges: 'Rosie writes to tell me that the Burial of poor old Tom went off well enough, and that his friends apparently took advantage of the absence of all the younger and revolutionary dons to elect as the new Provost a reactionary Hebrew called Jacquiz Helmutt.'

'Are those Rosie's terms?'

'No. She writes "moderate" and "civilized" for reactionary, and "Jew" for Hebrew. However, let us leave all that aside, and tell ourselves that we shall have a friend in the Provost's Lodging in Lancaster – for my old Gregory published several of Sir Helmutt's books – and that when Oenone comes to the right age (five or six, shall we say?) we could always ask for a free place for her at Lancaster Choir School.'

'The free places are reserved for the Choristers,' said Jo-Jo; 'and the Choristers are all boys.'

'Male chauvinist conspiracy. What's the matter with girls' voices?'

'They just don't do for sacred music,' said Jo-Jo: 'for sacred music you need men, boys or castrati.'

'I see. So girls are inferior even to castrati?' said Isobel furiously.

'It's no good blaming me, darling. They won't have them in any proper Choir, and that's all there is to it.'

'That's still no reason why Helmutt should not find Oenone a special scholarship of some kind.'

'There's no reason why he *should*. I'm stinking rich and everyone knows it.'

'Now you listen to me.' Isobel took her friend by the arm, wheeled her away from an up-ended thirteenth-century sarcophagus which she had been examining, and wrenched her across to the south side of the cloister, where they stood looking out on a small steep valley with a line of ilex on the opposite ridge.

'See those ilex?' said Isobel fiercely. 'They are healthy. When we first came here, there were treble the number, but two thirds of them were not healthy and had to be cut away. So it is with our money. Day by day it sickens and shrinks and the healthy core diminishes. You are not "stinking rich". You are "shrinking rich". By the time Oenone is old enough to go to Radigund's, if you decide to send her there, you may have almost nothing left. You may be *glad* that you saved the fee at the Choir School.'

'Very unlikely, old thing,' said Jo-Jo. 'I've got pots and pots. You don't half panic.'

'And another thing. It is immoral to pay fees for your daughter's education. It is *not* immoral to accept a free education for her at a fee-paying school.'

Jo-Jo laughed so much that she had to cling to a fluted column to stop herself reeling about, which would have been discourteous in a holy place and possibly unwise in one so macabre as this.

'Whoever pays,' she said at last, 'I like the idea of sending Oenone off to school in England at five or six. Sooner if possible.'

Oenone was lying in an open sarcophagus, a bad habit of hers that Rosie was always having to correct when she was there for the holidays.

'Oenone would like to go to school in England,' she announced from the depths of the stone coffin, 'if Rosie was there too.'

'Rosie would not be very far away,' said Jo-Jo, mendaciously.

'Oenone,' said Oenone, 'has two friends. One is Rosie and the other is Jeremy.'

'Jeremy?' said Isobel. 'Jeremy Morrison? But you haven't seen him, darling, in years.'

'Oenone remembers,' said Oenone. 'When Oenone was very little, Jeremy carried her and was kind to her in the back of Auntie Isobel's car.'

'But you were only *weeks* old,' said Jo-Jo. 'How can you remember?'

'Oenone remembers,' Oenone said.

She climbed out of the sarcophagus, took down her pants, perched herself on the side, and had a long splashy piddle on to the place where she had just been lying.

'Oenone remembers Jeremy put her on her potty,' Oenone said, getting down from the side of the sarcophagus and hauling up her knickers.

'All of this is quite true,' said Isobel: 'you remember that journey from Arles to Venice?⋆ Jeremy held her the whole way, so that you could sit in front…'

'And watch your legs, quivering over the gear stick of the Lagonda. I'll never forget it.'

'*And* he used to pot her, like she says.'

'Everyone here is kind to Oenone,' said Oenone; 'but all the same they want to send her away.'

'Only when you're old enough, darling,' said Isobel in a Judas voice, 'when you have to go away to school.'

'Will Jeremy or Rosie be there?' enquired Oenone.

'Perhaps not far away, darling,' lied Isobel; 'but we needn't think about all that just yet.'

'The sooner, the better,' whispered Jo-Jo to Isobel, hissing over the parapet and out into the valley. 'Surely there are places where they take them at three or four?'

'Only kindergarten,' said Isobel, 'from nine to noon. Not boarders. Besides, I think your good husband Jean-Marie would like to keep here for a while yet.'

'He's quite civil to her but he doesn't really notice her. He's much too involved in his book about this cathedral. I'll go and lug him out of the chancel. Time to go home. I've had enough of this spooky cloister.'

⋆ See *The Faces of the Waters*, by Simon Raven (*House of Stratus; 2001*).

'Oenone loves it,' Oenone said; 'all these pretty carvings, and the stone boxes *pour faire pi-pi.*'

'What you need,' said Jo-Jo, 'is children of your own age to play with, not carvings or stone boxes. We might think,' she said to Isobel, 'of a local French kindergarten? Even if it would only take her from nine to noon.'

'Low calibre parents in this part of the world,' Isobel said: 'Would you want to put her to school with the children of peasants and village shopkeepers – even if it was only from nine to noon?'

'Aren't you rather forgetting your new socialist principles, darling?'

'No, I'm not. Peasants and small shopkeepers are rural and reactionary. Now, if Oenone was going to be with the children of proper urban workers, I'd be all in favour.'

'I think,' said Jo-Jo, 'that consideration of this problem is tedious and best deferred.'

'Oenone thinks so too,' Oenone said.

Raisley Conyngham, knowing that he could never raise Milo from the depths of Trinity by telephone, and desiring (contrary to previous expectations) to alert him with some urgency, was discouraged to find that he could no longer send a telegram, since British Telecom considered such a proceeding to be retrograde to its intentions, but that he could send a thing called an 'Overnight Letter', which was much more modern and only took four or five times longer to get there.

'Marius suffering from infatuation,' dictated Raisley down his telephone: 'Heroine-worship plus phallus please investigate life and learning of Salinger of Lancaster and be ready to discuss.'

'No signature?' said the man at the exchange.

'He'll know who it's from.'

'What's all this "phallus" bit then? We're not allowed to transmit obscenities, you know.'

'Very well. Substitute "Priapus" for "phallus".'

'And who's Priapus when he's at home?'

'The God of Gardens,' said Raisley.

'Then why not say so in plain English?'

'Because it would be three words instead of one,' said Raisley, 'and I enjoy saving money.'

'Quite right, Guv; very good,' the man at the Exchange conceded. 'Don't let bloody British Telecom have it all their own way.'

Jacquiz Helmutt's information was (for once) out of date. Earle Restarick, the American agent, was no longer based in Constantinople but in Kyrenia on the north coast of Cyprus (which he much preferred). When he received Sir Jacquiz' letter, which had been swiftly redirected through service channels, he considered it more carefully than one would have expected of a hard man who had no time for flights of fantasy. This was because, fantastic as Helmutt's account of his children's disappearance might at first seem, Restarick knew that his correspondent was quite as hard-headed as he himself was and not the man to waste the time of either in speculation on the supernatural or paranormal. (Restarick, not having Latin or Greek, did not know how vile a hybrid the latter word was: even if he had known he would still have used it.)

Over the years Restarick had heard a good deal about Helmutt's twins and their origin and had even taken up the matter with Balbo Blakeney, who was associated with the events that had led to their begetting, and to whom Sir Jacquiz had introduced him. As a scientist, Blakeney inclined to the view that the twins were sports or mutants of some kind – and there, perforce, he stopped. And there, thought Restarick, we all stop.

He wrote now to Helmutt to say that he was prepared (as one doing a favour which would be duly accounted as such) to send him a false report on the twins' monthly progress in Cyprus, in order to satisfy any busybody who might later enquire into their whereabouts; and that for the rest he would gladly keep an eye open for the errant couple, with whom he would be most interested to communicate were they in a mood to communicate with him. However, he continued, the Levant (for which Sir Jacquiz thought the twins to be bound) was a comprehensive area geographically, and he (Restarick) was doubtful whether the twins would be visiting Kyrenia for whatever purpose. But yet again, the area was prolific in historical remains, notably those of Crusaders and the monastic military orders – souvenirs of a type which (he understood) might somehow concern the twins and might therefore bring them to the island. He would, at any rate, keep watch.

Restarick concluded with his congratulations on Helmutt's elevation to the Provost's Throne (his own hyperbole), of which he had been apprised quite independently, and with a request that Helmutt would disseminate his good wishes to such of their common acquaintance as were liable to visit Lancaster, foremost among them Major Fielding Gray, the Lord Canteloupe (whom he had known as Detterling) and Canteloupe's private secretary, Leonard Percival; for Restarick did not know that Percival was now too broken ever to move away from Canteloupe's house in Wiltshire.

Earl Restarick then thought, very briefly, of his Lancaster friend, Daniel Mond, now some years dead, whom he had long ago betrayed. He pursed his thin, curving lips as he remembered the gaudy spring in Göttingen, nearly a generation past, the walks in the morning valleys and the evening forests, and the innocent affection they had shared before he had been compelled to turn against Daniel. After all, he thought, that was the condition of our friendship – that if necessary I should later betray it. No love; no betrayal: no betrayal, no love. Every dream has its price. He remembered those lines that Leonard Percival had been so fond of quoting:

If there were dreams to sell,
Merry and sad to tell,
And the crier rang the bell,
What would you buy?

Milo knew Carmilla Salinger, whom he had met when staying with the former Provost during the summer, and he knew that she detested him. Nothing was to be gained by going to see her in person: she would simply throw him out. So instead he went to see Len, whom Sir Jacquiz Helmutt had prudently retained as Provost's Private Secretary (much to the pleasure of Marigold, who had once had a luscious, steamy 'thing' with Len, which, though it had long since dried in the wind [so to speak], had left her with a pleasant residual itch for him). Len had been at least polite to Milo during his stay at the Lodging, was indeed grateful to him (Milo realized) for amusing the Provost as he tottered toward the shadowy coast and might assist him now.

'Carmilla Salinger,' Milo came straight out with her name to him: 'is she a serious lady?'

'Why should you ask?' said Len, wondering whether his combination of pink velvet tie and green knickerbockers with tartan stockings (Gordon) had not been, even for him, overdoing it.

'Apparently,' said Milo Hedley, 'she is having a walk-out with Marius Stern.'

'It was always on the cards.'

'Certainly. But several friends of Marius are anxious. He has a lot to attend to at School this quarter, and must sit his O Levels at the end of it. We don't want him disturbed or distracted.'

They went into the garden of the Lodging and sat down on a seat, presented to the late Provost by Lord Luffham of Whereham, which had Jeremy Morrison's name and dates at the College carved on it.

'He's better off shagging Carmilla when they can get together,' said Len, 'than shagging his School sheets. Or perhaps he'll do both. None of which can do much harm.'

'Unless she...diddles him.'

'She won't do that. Carmilla never diddled anybody, in any sense. She plays straight. She won't let Marius down, boy, don't you worry about that.'

And that is what Milo told Raisley Conyngham, a day or two later, as they watched the School XI play its first footer match of the season on the hill above Farncombe Valley.

'Yes,' said Conyngham, who was wearing a Free Foresters' Cricket Blazer with a (passably smart) Regimental tie, khaki jodhpurs and chukka boots: 'yes, that makes very good sense. Those Salinger girls don't let people down.'

'From which it follows, sir,' said Milo, 'that if one were having an affair with Miss Carmilla, with loyal, honest, generous, kind and caring Miss Carmilla – '

' – *Caring*, Milo? – '

' – Sorry, sir: a nasty piece of modern jargon meaning "considerate", more or less the equivalent of the odious "compassionate" – '

' – I see. Carry on, Milo – '

' – As I was about to say, sir, it must follow that anyone who was enjoying the warm and genuine affections of Miss Carmilla, and then in some significant way deliberately cheated or deceived her, anyone who did that, sir, would be conspicuously violating every criterion of decency and honour.'

'Indeed. But we do not wish Marius to be conspicuous for such violation.'

'Certainly not, sir, nor he need be. UP, UP, UP, SCHOOL. CENTRE, CENTRE, CENTRE. Sorry, sir. You may remember that I was quite keen on footer.'

'One of your more wholesome attributes, Milo. You were saying...that there is no reason why Marius' treachery should be conspicuous.'

'None at all, sir.' Milo smiled his special smile, carefully copied from that of a marble Delian kouros of the Archaic period. 'No one else need know of it save us.'

'And have you thought of any useful purpose such a betrayal might serve? A bonus is always useful, Milo.'

Half-time. The teams sucked lemons. Milo and Raisley paced the touchline, watched by admiring boys, who saw a rich man furnished with ability and accompanied by his grateful and distinguished pupil.

'There would be an agreeable bonus for me, sir. And for you, the additional satisfaction that this act of betrayal would be compounded by the most vile ingratitude toward someone other than Miss Carmilla.'

'Expound,' said Raisley, adopting a cavalry stance.

'Consider, sir, the case of Jeremy Morrison. Through the good offices of Miss Carmilla and her sister Canteloupe, Jeremy has been despatched by the publishers Salinger, Stern & Detterling on a mission at once romantic and redemptive. The press has proclaimed it, the television sets of the nation have vibrated with it. The Honble Jeremy Morrison, disgraced leader of the "Back to the Earth Mother" movement, of which many had such hopes – Jeremy Morrison, having soiled his soul with Sodomy Down Under, is sailing out to cleanse it in the waves of the never-resting sea. Accompanied by Fielding Gray, he is to sail West from Ithaca as Odysseus might once have sailed, on and on through the Pillars of Hercules, out into the Great Ocean and so to the edge of the world itself, unless he is fortunate enough to come first to the Isles of the Blessèd where is the Shrine (or so at least the columnist Alfie Schroeder assures us) of the Holy Grail.'

'Have you any objection to their taking such a cruise?'

'I am intrigued by Jeremy, sir. Jeremy and I have a piquant and highly gratifying relation. Intermittent though this necessarily is, I do not wish it interrupted for the time it would take him to find the Holy Grail. Nor do I wish him to perish in the attempt. In a word, I want him back. Not tomorrow nor even next week...but certainly before he reaches the Pillars of Hercules.'

'If Jeremy Morrison is your idea of a bonus, Milo, so be it. I must own that he has his attractions – or did when he was at this School. As to the aspect of betrayal, I think I see your drift. Only Carmilla Salinger or Theodosia Canteloupe, the patronesses of this expedition, can bring him back. And why should they want to do that, unless persuaded by someone? And who better to persuade either of them – though we are now thinking largely of Carmilla – than Marius Stern, her page and lover –?'

' – Right, sir. UP, UP, SCHOOL – '

' – Her page and lover, who would thus be manipulating Carmilla into recalling the very man whom she herself sent forth with her favours, so to speak, fastened to his helm. In this way Marius would be exploiting his fond and true-hearted mistress by deceiving or otherwise coercing her into subverting the gallant mission of a friend – not only her friend but his, and one to whom he owes a great sum of gratitude over the years. A double dose of treachery. Ingenious, Milo.'

'The lucubrations of an apprentice, sir. It will take you, the master, to apply them. UP SCHOOL, UP SCHOOL, RIGHT UP SCHOOL.'

'Quite so. Go back to Cambridge and into residence at Trinity, Milo. Mind your book, and do nothing else whatever until you hear further from me. Meanwhile, I shall converse with Marius.'

'Very good, sir. UP, UP, UP, UP, RIGHT UP SCHOOL.'

Jeremy Morrison and Fielding Gray flew to Corfu and hired a car to Ermones on the west coast.

'This is where Odysseus was washed ashore,' Fielding said, 'and later encountered Nausikaa.'

'Not all scholars are agreed on the location.'

'All men of taste are,' Fielding said.

They walked down the track from the car park to the beach itself.

'He must have slept up here in the scrub,' Fielding said. 'Nausikaa and her girls, coming from the north, would have arrived down the opposite bank of the river with the laundry wagon. There are the natural tanks for them to do their laundry in, there is the beach on which to dry it and to play ball while it is drying, and there is the estuary channel into which one of them threw their beautiful ball by mistake – and set the rest squealing so loudly that Odysseus was woken and came down by the way we are coming down now. We worked it all out when I was doing the script for that film of the Odyssey in 1970.'*

'How charming,' Jeremy beamed out of his full moon face and shambled down the path with his loose, long-limbed walk. 'And what did you do about that commodious hotel over there? Can it be called The Nausikaa? But of course. And all these delicious people with such appetizing pink torsoes, who are, no doubt, staying in it? Did you pay them to keep off the beach?'

'None of this was there then.'

'I wonder,' said Jeremy, 'how many of them know the story of Odysseus. Should one of us strip off and make an entrance like he did? Starkers, except for a titillating olive branch. All Nausikaa's girls had fits of hysteria, I recall. I wonder what these good people would do? Just gape, I expect. Indeed they all seem to be gaping anyway. Is that what they've come all the way to Corcyra for? Just to gape?'

* See *Come Like Shadows*, by Simon Raven (*Blond & Briggs; 1972*).

'At least,' said Fielding, shading his one eye, 'they appear to be harmless. They are not drunk, and they are queuing in an orderly fashion for their hamburgers.'

'That is because they are the September tourists,' said Jeremy, who had paused by the tanks: 'comparatively quiet and sensible people who have decided to avoid the crush. But even in September they are far from perfect. You may have noticed, as we came through the town, those gangs of young men on motorcycles – '

' – Probably Greeks – '

' – No. Even nastier and more aggressive, indisputably British, sporting some form of football colours. The motorbikes were hired, you see. What on earth are they doing here anyway?'

'Exacting their return for the mean and subordinate roles dished out to them by their lot. Their price is a temporary pretension to freedom and equality. They will lead their dreary lives and do their dreary work for fifty weeks in the year provided that for the other two they are allowed to think that they are free and equal with you and me. Provided they are allowed to come to the same places,' said Fielding, grinning through his thin pink plastic mouth, 'they will be more or less content. The fact that they do not know where they are, in historical or even geographical terms, and would just as soon, in fact far sooner, be in Southend given fair weather, is beside the point. They want to have the illusion of being like you and me and the pleasure of vexing us with their horrible accents and uncouth ubiquity.'

'What do you suppose Odysseus would have made of this lot here?' said Jeremy, swivelling his bland gaze over the beach.

'If he'd had his ship with him, he'd have herded them up like cattle, killed the hopelessly old and infirm, and sold the rest of them as slaves, keeping one or two of the more delectable for himself. If, on the other hand, he'd been alone, he would have erected a stall for the sale of pizza and dirty mags.'

'Oh dear. To think that I'm to step into his shoes when we get to Ithaca.'

'I'm making it easy for you. You are no hero, my dear, and neither was Odysseus; his shoes will fit you the easier for that. He was always blundering and blubbering and being crapulously self indulgent – just like you. He had his moments of dignity, of course, as you do – dignity which he often compromised by giggling or farting. In one thing, however, you do differ: he'd have known exactly what to do about the crowd here – sell them something, or start sucking up to them until he'd cadged enough to be off. *You* do *not* know what to do about them, like me you're quite appalled by them, innocent and inoffensive as most of them really are, and so I suggest we return to the town, seek the harbour and get on with our journey without further delay.'

'But before we go,' said Jeremy, 'answer me this. You have spoken, up to a point, in their defence. But surely you cannot forgive them for desecrating the Princess Nausikaa's beach?'

'I recently purchased some shares in something called Scheria Kerkyra Holidays,' said Fielding. 'The Nausikaa Hotel is our prize money spinner. One cannot have it both ways.'

From Corfu they took a boat, the next morning, to the Port of Vathi (Deep) in Ithaca. Here they hired a taxi which carried them by the vertiginous road north along the ridge to Stavros. Stavros stood at the neck of a re-entrant that descended, from the plateau on which the little town was built, to a narrow creek and a natural harbour. In the harbour was a small white motor launch with a tall mast. It had been procured and paid for by Salinger, Stern & Detterling, whose agent, a bald, stocky man who wore the bottoms of his trousers rolled, was there to demonstrate the working of the engine, show them where the stores (including emergency fuel) and the necessary charts were stowed, and explain the harbour procedures and forms of custom clearance to be followed both within and when leaving

Greek waters. The boat carried a painted eye on either side of the bow, but there was no sign of a name.

'Like Odysseus when in the cave of the Cyclops,' the agent explained: ' "Nobody" he called himself, the "Nameless One".'

'Why the mast?'

The stocky man shrugged.

'Symbolic,' Fielding said. 'I notice that we have exactly the space which you were offered. A single bunk, a single chair, and a very small table hinged to the wall. One of us can eat or sleep or play patience while the other watches above.'

He did not mention, in front of the representative, that they intended to spend all nights ashore.

Due west of Stavros and about two miles away across a channel, on the east coast of Cephalonia, was Huiscardo, named for Robert the Guiscard, famous for its lobsters.

'We might spend tomorrow night there,' said Jeremy when the agent had gone.

'Too slack. Only two miles in one day?'

'Carmilla said I wasn't to hurry. "It's the journey that counts," she said, "as much as the quest or the discovery. Better not get there at all than get there too soon." I'll tell you what. We can spin out the journey across the channel by mooring at that little island, halfway across, with the hermitage on it.'

'It looks…no more than a strip of rock.'

'Good test of my seamanship,' said Jeremy. 'I *was* a Sea Cadet at School, you know.'

'So you have told me. Do you think anyone lives in that hermitage?'

Local enquiry that evening elicited that the hermitage was uninhabited but that the chapel, little more in size than a sentry-box, was visited and blessed once a year. There was, the town know-all told them, a tiny beach of shingle on the other side of the islet.

'It would be funny,' said Jeremy, as The Nameless One purred slowly out of the creek at a comfortable hour the next morning, 'if we found the Grail in that chapel after only one hour's sailing.'

But all there was in the chapel was an orange and yellow hooped bathing-costume, which, if worn, would have stretched from neck to knees, hanging on the wall between a battered eikon and a broken cross.

'The MCC colours,' Fielding said: 'surely a good omen. Someone must have hung it there in dedication…out of gratitude, perhaps, for an escape from the sea. When this voyage is done, we must find a shrine and do the same.'

Both of them knelt before the orange and yellow bathing-costume and prayed to the God of Ocean, to Poseidon the Earth-Shaker, that has all sailors in his hand. Then they sailed on to Huiscardo, where they were welcomed with a large, stale and astronomically priced lobster, and lodged in small, damp beds. On the next morning, driven forth by the thronging fauna in the blankets at a more nautical hour than that at which they had embarked the previous day, they veered east round the northern cape of Ithaca and set course for Missalonghi.

'Depressing start for the West,' remarked Jeremy, 'heading north-east.'

'But necessary. We both know that. We could never have trusted ourselves to cross open sea to Sicily or Taranto. Anyhow,' said Fielding, 'as you keep saying, Carmilla deprecates haste. Stick to the coast and we'll come to little harm.'

At Missalonghi, where they spent the night, everything was much nastier than at Huiscardo, as there were no lobsters, not even stale ones, and lots of smelly black swamps.

'The Albanian Coast,' said Fielding over their rebarbative supper, 'may be a problem. *They* won't like the cut of our jib.'

'We'll see about that when we get there. The Albanians are subject to the same maritime law as anyone else.'

'And have made up one or two extra, I dare say.'

But they took heart, because the next day their real voyage would begin, north by Dubrovnik and Split and Trieste, south again along the leg of Italy, round the heel and toe and so past Sicily, then up the west coast of Italy and along the south coast of France, by then at last well set (were the gods willing) in the western way which they must follow, until at last they came to the Pillars of Hercules and the Great Ocean that encircles the earth.

PART TWO

The Tip of the Arrow

Love is winsome at the start:
Yet once you let His arrow's tip
Lightliest prick or cheek or lip
Soon the whole shaft shall cleave your heart.

From the Greek of Paulus Silentarius
Translated by S R

Raisley conyngham took Marius Stern for a walk along the path by the river at the bottom of Farncombe Hill.

'The papers,' remarked Raisley, 'have a lot to say about this voyage of your friend Jeremy Morrison with Fielding Gray.'

'It is Carmilla Salinger's way of setting up Jeremy after that horrid business in Australia.'

'Oh? Why should she show such interest...in setting up a young man who is almost as rich as she is?'

'There is more than money in it, sir. Carmilla has always been keen on Jeremy. So has her sister, if in rather a different way. They think he has been going to pot, and now they want to pull him together.'

'Do *you* think he has been going to pot, Marius? You were always close to him.'

'I might have been when he was there, sir. He hasn't been around much just lately.'

'No,' said Raisley Conyngham: 'he hasn't. And now it looks as if he won't be for some considerable time to come.'

A light breeze rattled in the sedge between the path and the river.

'Well,' said Marius: 'I couldn't have gone with him, and that's that. He said that he would have taken me if I could have done.'

'But of course that was impossible, so he took Fielding Gray instead. You still haven't answered my question, Marius. Do you think Jeremy Morrison has been going to pot?'

'I think...that he is too easygoing.'

'Will Fielding Gray stiffen him up? On this expedition?'

'I think so, sir. Fielding being older, will be able to be much tougher with him than I could have been. Besides, Jeremy has always admired Fielding's methods of dealing with life and its difficulties.'

'In a word, then, they will not mind about you. You are superfluous.'

'If you care to put it like that, sir.'

'Just like that, Marius. And what is more you will remain superfluous. Very soon they will cease to think of you at all.'

'They will have a lot else to think about; but I don't think they will forget me altogether.'

'Not at first. But the days will go on, Marius, and sooner or later they will come to the land or the island of which Odysseus dreamed when he left Ithaca, for the second time, this time to sail, not to Troy, but to the West. Apparently Jeremy has promised to seek until he finds what Odysseus was seeking. It seems that he will know it when he sees it. It must be…something rather tremendous, Marius. Do you think that there will be room in his life both for it and for you?'

They came to a small, green boathouse on the bank. Raisley Conyngham unlocked a side door. Inside, a rowing boat was floating in a creek which lapped right into the boathouse itself, under the river gates. In the dim light, Conyngham unfastened these and opened them outward.

'You row, Marius. I shall steer.'

'What a jolly little boat, sir. What's she called?'

'She has no name. Just row, Marius. Upstream. We shall not go far. As I was saying…when Jeremy Morrison comes to the land or the island which will offer him what Odysseus sought on his last voyage, will he have room left in his life for you?'

'With respect, sir, you exaggerate.' Marius rowed steadily into the gentle current. 'This whole thing is a literary stunt, to distract Jeremy and give him healthy occupation. Sooner or later he may find something of interest and write about his search, with or without the help of Fielding Gray; but let us not inflate the thing. He is not going to see a Light or a Vision or a Mystery. We both know that. He is not going to be so dazzled as to be blind to old friends.'

'A man sees a Vision, Marius, not because the Vision is there, but because he yearns for one.'

'Jeremy yearns for no Vision.'

'Does he not? What about all this Cult of the Earth Mother?'

'A spoof, sir. To test the folly of the human race.'

'So. In your view, Jeremy Morrison will not see any Vision or find any Marvel among the Isles of the Blessèd or the Blest? Nothing that will change himself or his existing affections? Let us turn the boat, Marius...right blade only while I work on the rudder...that's it. Now ship your oars and we can drift back. Has it occurred to you, Marius, that even if Visions do not exist, they can be manufactured? And then they are seen even by people who do not yearn for them. Carmilla and her sister have sent Jeremy on a quest: perhaps it is just a literary stunt, as you say; or perhaps, having gone to such trouble and expense, they will be anxious that he should find something of commensurate significance.'

'If they put it there, it will still be part of the stunt.'

'But if it is something unusual yet plausible? Something amazing or at least attractive? And if his imagination works on it?'

'Your drift, sir, if you please?'

'That Carmilla may be jealous of your affection for Jeremy or of Jeremy's affection for you. At the very least, she may want to keep you in separate compartments. Women are very odd creatures, Marius, even the sanest of them. Whatever else Carmilla and her sister are trying to distract Jeremy from, one or both of them may be trying to distract him from you.'

'But I have told you, sir. I have hardly seen Jeremy for a very long time.'

'But you saw a lot of him once. And you were going to again, Marius. He had invited you out to Australia for a holiday.'

'Yes, sir.'

'But he was arrested before you could go, and there was an end of that. Yet Carmilla may be looking forward and thinking to herself that such invitation could well be given another time, and that this time nothing, probably, would prevent your enjoying it...that this time you and Jeremy might be off somewhere without her, without thinking or even thinking of her.'

'We are near your boathouse, sir.'

'Let the boat drift on. We will take it to Banham's on Farncombe Quay, where it will be laid up for the winter.'

'Very good... So, sir, you are telling me that Carmilla and her sister, Lady Canteloupe, may be planning to put some violent or impressive surprise in Jeremy's way that would altogether detach his attention from myself. Presumably... *you take a view...* of this matter. What is it?'

'You grow too direct, Marius. As usual, I wish to suit my own convenience and that of as many of my friends as possible. It has occurred to me, and to Milo, that we do not wish Jeremy Morrison to be so exclusively controlled by these two sisters, and that therefore we should like him back in England before he can come on whatever they have devised for him to come on.'

'Too late. Jeremy and Fielding are now at sea.'

'Not too late if Carmilla or Theodosia could be induced to send for them, to order them back...under threat of withdrawing support.'

'They would have to find them first. In any case, why *should* Carmilla order them back?'

'I thought you might find a reason for her, Marius. And put it to her when you next visit her in Lancaster. You say she intends to...continue...with you. Make her love you, Marius. Make her unable to refuse your request.'

'You command this, sir?'

'I do, Marius.'

'Then I shall obey. You know that. Quite why I shall obey, I do not know: yet obey I shall, and gladly. I wish to be commanded by you.'

'You shall also be rewarded. You remember when you were rewarded with Jenny, Marius?'

'I remember.' Marius turned his head. 'Here is Banham's,' he announced.

'I shall steer us in. You will never again be rewarded with Jenny. This time, and all the times that are to come, your reward will be far more precious and far more subtle than she could ever be.'

'How long do you give me, sir? To persuade Carmilla?'

'It will be no good, I think, trying to rush or force her. You must take your time and respect her person.'

'I think time is on our side, sir. Jeremy and Fielding will sail only along the coast. It will take them a very long while to reach the Isles of the Blessèd – or the Blest. We should be able to catch up with them well before that. I am to visit Carmilla next during the School's first Petty Absit in mid-October.'

'Soon enough, Marius the Egyptian: soon enough.'

In the little port of Cassiopi on the east coast of Corfu, Fielding and Jeremy sat down to consider the problem of negotiating Albanian waters. Albania was only a mile or two away from them, across a narrow strait. As long as they were in the strait, and kept well over towards the Corfiot shore, all would be well. But when Corfu fell behind them to the south; there was no way of knowing how distant the regulations or the whims of the Albanians might require them to steer while pursuing their passage north.

So now they sat outside a café under the ruined Venetian Fort and on the edge of the northern quay, and pondered the matter.

'Local knowledge needed,' said Fielding: 'as simple as that.'

Cretinous lobster-skinned Britons went waddling and whining past their table, having no local knowledge nor any other. A bald, red-faced man, in fawn slacks and pukkha desert boots and sporting an insolent Elizabethan sea-captain's beard, put both his hands on Fielding's shoulders.

'*Res Unius, Res Omnium,*' he said. 'Cornet Julian James rises from your past to salute you.'

He kissed Fielding on his pink plastic forehead.

'Julian. Oh Julian. How did you recognize me? It has been so long and my face has been blown to pieces since you saw me last.'

'I read about that. A bomb in Cyprus, they said. Luckily your hair is still the same – an odd shade of amber and two pretty waves over the ears.'

'Oh. My hair…Julian, this is my friend, Jeremy Morrison.'

'Ah. The Earth Mother man. The Greek papers got very keen about you. I have followed your career with interest.'

'All of it?'

'Most of it. I'll bet Ozzy slammers aren't as beastly as Greek ones.'

'When were you in a Greek prison, Julian?' Fielding asked him.

'Any time these last fifteen years…for saying nasty things about the Colonels when they were in and nice things about them when they were thrown out.'

'I wonder they didn't throw you out.'

'I have a Greek passport. My dear, I own a little villa just down the coast. Inherited from my mother, whose father was a Corfiot.'

'You live here? What happened to you, Julian, when you left the Regiment?'

'Fielding and I,' explained Julian James to Jeremy, 'were in something called the 10th Sabre Squadron in Goettingen in the early 'fifties. Fielding commanded. I obeyed. I didn't mind obeying Fielding. What he asked was usually quite reasonable in the circs, and he asked in a civil manner. The trouble was that when I was demobilized I couldn't learn to obey anyone else. Rubbish it all was: rubbish employing rubbish to supervise rubbish in the manufacture of rubbish for the consumption of rubbish – the modern world in a nutshell. So I came to Greece, where exactly the same thing was happening, but here the process hadn't gone quite so far and didn't make quite such a noise and stink; and in any case the villa which I'd inherited from Mama was very remote. Agios Andreas.'

'It can hardly be so remote now,' said Jeremy, watching an ovoid female colossus as she slapped a skeletal and yowling infant on its twiggy thighs and told it to 'yeigh oop'. 'Do you suppose that woman *can* have dropped that brat?'

'You will see nothing of the kind in Agios Andreas,' said Cornet Julian James. 'There is my house over the beach, and a Church (surprisingly large) over my house, and four fishermen's shacks scattered among the rocks under the cliff. So we cannot fill the Church. Two more will be welcome tomorrow, which is Sunday, you may remember. Stay the weekend: stay forever. There are many books and an ample cellar and a great peace. The Priest and I have put it about that there are vampires in the vicinity – as indeed there are, come to that – and have managed to scare off the tourist agencies, who were about to erect some bungalows.'

'They can't have believed that business about the vampires.'

'There were difficulties in convincing them. The real vampires were sulking at the time – they often do, you know, very temperamental – so the Priest had to take on the job. Not a nice one. Greek vampires, as you may know, do not suck blood: they batter their victims to bits. One nosy female agent battered to bits by the Priest soon settled the rest of 'em. They haven't been seen since.'

'The Police must have been seen since?'

'Oh no. The Corfiot Police understand their limitations. They fully realize that they are not up to vampires...who, however, sanguinary and temperamental as they are, will not interfere with any guests of mine. So come and stay for a long time. We can talk together of the old days, Fielding, and of what happened to Daniel Mond.★ We can talk of prisons, Jeremy, and exchange penological titbits. Not that they ever kept me very long. They were afraid the vampires wouldn't like it and might come to rescue me.'

'We are sailing westward,' said Fielding, 'for the Isles of the Blest, and we may not linger long, since we follow the coast and our course is devious.'

'Then I shall guide you for a while and save you much labour and many days. At one time or another I have sailed all the Dalmatian Coast. Where is your vessel? Can you find room for me?'

Jeremy pointed.

'No name,' he said. 'There is room for you providing we put ashore every night. We were fussed about Albania. No putting ashore there, I think.'

'None,' said Julian James. 'We shall go to my grandfather's island instead. "Philomela" it is called. Ten easy hours north-by-west will take us to it, and from there to the coast of Yugoslavia is only an eight-hour run.'

'You have a house there too? On the island?'

'You will see what I have. Tonight and Sunday night here, I think; the Priest will never forgive me if I do not bring you to his Church tomorrow, as he adores celebrities. Then the sea – Philomela – Illyria. You can take me as far as Dubrovnik, if you will. I can walk home from there.'

'It might take some time?'

★ See *The Sabre Squadron*, by Simon Raven *(Anthony Blond Ltd; 1966)*.

'I have nothing else to do,' said Julian James, 'and nobody except the Priest and the vampires will miss me.'

'Cora Corrington's chums,' said Len to Sir Jacquiz Helmutt as they sat drinking tea by the river on the lawn of Jacquiz' villa at Grantchester, 'are planning to make a bigger row than we thought.'

'What kind of row?' said Marigold' Helmutt, putting down a covered dish. 'First crumpets of the season,' she said. 'What are Cora's little friends up to?'

'They are not her friends,' said Jacquiz: 'they have wished themselves on to her in order to exploit her name and her conveniently situated rooms.'

'Trouble is,' said Len, 'she has no way of wishing them off her – short of shooting them, and poor Cora ain't up to firearms. And so they are doing exactly what they set out to do. Exploiting her name and her rooms to assemble their forces – who are now to stage a protest, not just against the ethnic ratio of the College, but against the methods we used to get you elected as Provost. They are also co-opting Fellows of the College as they drift back from their vacations.'

'One would have thought that the Fellows of the College,' said Jacquiz, 'would wait until they could convene the College Council in a few days' time and then complain through the proper channels.'

'They can't,' said Len, biting off half a crumpet and masticating with open mouth in time to the emission of his words: 'the College Visitor has already confirmed your Election as being legitimate in the existing emergency.'

'The College Visitor,' said Marigold, 'is the Lord Bishop of Ely. No friend of Jacquiz. How did you persuade him?'

'The Bishop is away,' said Len. 'The same principle applies to the confirmation of the Election as did to the Election itself. The Senior Fellow (in the continued absence of the Vice-Provost) is empowered to act for the Visitor, whom he has already represented, in case application to the Visitor finds him still unavailable. I took care that this should be the case. So you are now elected and confirmed,' he said to Sir Jacquiz (having first thrust in the other half of his crumpet), 'with and by the authority of the Visitor − the Senior Fellow's signature being stamped and sealed with the Bishop's Intaglio, a copy of which is kept here, in a special cabinet, for his use when in residence.'

'Was that fair play?' asked Marigold.

'Yes. The Bishop holds the key to this cabinet which holds this copy of his Intaglio. If he entrusts the key to the Provost or Vice-Provost, they are entitled to use it at their discretion. His Lordship, who is a close man, had of course entrusted it to nobody − simply mislaid it,' said Len, 'when last he was here. It was − er − found by the Bedmaker of the Episcopal Guest Suite; she entrusted it to me; I meant to return it to His Lordship, but, under pressure of this and that, forgot to do so. I was therefore able to pass it to the Senior Fellow, the legitimate representative of the absent Vice-Provost who is the legitimate representative of the absent Visitor − I was, I say, able and entitled to pass the key direct to the Senior Fellow, present when all else were absent, who had need of it to confirm and ratify the emergency Election.'

'*Not* fair play,' Marigold said.

'But not to be faulted,' said Len: 'for the fouls are far too slick to admit of proof. As far as we are concerned, the Bishop left the key to the Intaglio Cabinet here in our keeping, knowing that he would be much absent and wishing the copy of the Intaglio to be readily available to his licit representatives…who in the event turned out to be solely the Honourable Grantchester FitzMargrave Pough, Senior Fellow of Lancaster. End of argument.'

'But not end of protest,' Marigold said. 'Have the last crumpet, Len.'

Len had it.

'So,' said Sir Jacquiz: 'Cora Corrington's feminist and anti-racialist acquaintance, or rather; her deceased aunt's, plus a group of Fellows, male and female, now returned to the College, are to stage a demonstration which, I apprehend, could be violent and even armed, to protest against the preponderance of whites in the College and also against the manner of my own Election as Provost.'

'Right,' said Len.

'When?'

'On the day of your Induction.'

'They will use Cora's rooms as their HQ?'

'Precisely.'

'Although,' said Jacquiz, 'Cora wants nothing to do with any of it?'

'Cora wants only to be left in peace with *Bufo Aegyptianus*,' said Len. 'I have brought pressure on the Head of her Faculty, who has a personal weakness so revolting that I must not mention it in front of Marigold, to send her on an expedition to the Nile to collect live specimens of a reported rogue variant. Cora's Flight into Egypt began this morning with her departure to Heathrow in a taxi at five a.m. This leaves us free to take certain precautions.'

'Like closing up Cora's rooms?'

'No,' said Len: 'like *not* closing up Cora's rooms. They'd only find others to use as a base before the day of the Induction. We much prefer to know where they are. So full preparations have been made for the provision, promised under duress by Cora, of all such nutriments, articles and services as were required of her. Her chambers will still be their rallying point.'

'Will they resent her defection?'

'Not much. They'll attribute it to urgent work for humanity. Cleverly tricked banners for Cora's cause will be much more impressive than ever Cora could have been.'

'So where is our advantage?'

'Cora may not much care for her associates, Provost, but she has a soft heart and a humane conscience. These are now with her in Egypt.'

'So what are you going to *do*?' said Marigold, and licked melted butter off her fingers. 'To protect old Jacquiz here? And yourself, for that matter? And the rest of the College?'

'Just wait and see, darling,' said Len: 'it'll be much more exciting like that, now won't it?'

As the north west angle of Corfu and then the Orthoni islands sank beneath the horizon, Julian James said,

'The fishermen at Agios Andreas say that there will be calm for another three days.'

Soon after, since they had for some time been sailing almost due west, the mountains of Albania flickered and set.

'Open sea,' said Julian. 'Make new course: due north for Philomela.'

Open sea, thought Fielding, as all three of them clustered round the wheel on the tiny bridge. In a toy boat, at the mercy of the Mediterranean – never mind what Julian's fisherfolk might have said about calm weather. The fiercest lightning always came from a clear sky. I wish my old grandfather could see me now, he thought. He always despised the cowardice which he knew was lurking just beneath my dainty skin. If he could have seen me now he might have taken a bit back.

Fielding thought of his book about the old man, about his strength, his splendour, his ignorance, his contempt for the cultured pursuits of his grandson. There were two volumes of this book: first, *The Grand Grinder*, now published some weeks since, about the old man's sporting youth and his brave days in the Yeomanry; and then, *The Master Baker*, due out in early November, an account of his surly middle-age, through which he conscientiously supervised the Cambridge Bakery he had inherited and caused its fine bread to be punctually delivered to the Colleges, while all the time yearning for the Column and the Trumpet, escaping whenever possible to watch horses run at Brampton or on Newmarket Heath. It was during the latter period that he had come to know and to despise the grandson who admired him so much. Well, thought Fielding: I have praised the soldier and the sportsman, and I have defended myself against the carping strictures of the peevish and arthritic pantaloon; justice and duty have been done to his memory without inflated adulation of his prowess or undue resentment of his philistine petulance. RIP.

But would the two volumes command either sales, he wondered, or critical respect? Probably neither: the matter was little to the taste of an indoor public of state-subsidized hypochondriacs and envy-ridden pen-pushers; while the critics would deplore the elitist achievements of the grand grinder himself and Fielding's elitist comments on his intellectual deficiencies. Well, thought Fielding: as to money, that deal with Canteloupe over the Albani manuscript has set me right for a good while to come; and as for critical accolade or damnation, I shall not be open to anything in either line during this new Odyssey.

'The Priest,' Julian was saying, 'took a liking to you two at yesterday's luncheon after the Service. He says that while you have both seen through God, you are courteous enough to pay Him the deference due to a Veteran. He has therefore composed a suitable prayer for us to recite when in the open sea.'

'He sympathized with me,' said Fielding, 'because man has ruined my face nearly as cruelly as God has botched his body.'

'You'd be surprised how many of the local nuns go for him,' said Julian: 'something to do with his hump. And of course his being almost a midget gives them a motherly glow – often the preface to an erotic flare.'

'What's this prayer he has written?' Jeremy enquired.

' "A thought recommended to those on an empty sea under an empty sky," ' read Julian from a scrap of paper which he brought out of his pocket: ' "You are now clear of all sight of imbecile humanity and its vile habitation, and I understand that you are promised fair weather. What then can offend you, you may ask, or what harrass you? Beware, my friends: no man is ever safe from the ubiquitous malice of God." '

'I was just thinking much the same,' Fielding said. 'Bolts from the blue, that kind of a thing.'

'There is more,' said Julian James. ' "Do not forget, however, should this malice assail you, that it is through His malice that God often expresses His love. For even now, old and weary as God may be, he deprecates sloth or atrophy in those whom He loves and is therefore often minded to goad them into vigour while leaving the rump of the race to wallow and stew in the vapour of its own corruption." '

'Rather overdone towards the end?' said Jeremy.

'I don't know,' said Julian. 'Would Donne have disowned the passage? I am rather proud of my pupil. He has his English from me, you see – and the run of my library. In return he shows me complete devotion in most things, though I fear lest he disapproves of my fondness for the island of Philomela. He is jealous, pettish and suspicious whenever I so much as mention it.'

'With good reason, perhaps,' remarked Jeremy. 'Philomela was the sister of Procne that was the wife of Tereus. Tereus desired Philomela and ravished her; then tore out her tongue lest she should communicate this misadventure. However, she then wove the story into a web, and showed it to Procne, who thereupon killed and cooked her offspring by Tereus (a son called Ithys) and served him up in a ragout to his father. Somehow Tereus recognized the flavour and drew his sword to slaughter all present – but at this stage he himself was transformed into a hoopoe, his wife, Procne, into a nightingale, and Philomela into a swallow.'

'Not *entirely* correct,' said Julian James. 'In the version told by the Latin poets, Procne was turned into a swallow and Philomela into a nightingale.'

'Such rubbish,' said Jeremy. 'How could the nightingale sing when its tongue had been torn out?'

'Perhaps,' said Fielding, 'its voice was restored by whatever divine power engineered the transformation? What power, by the way? Do we know?'

'We might if we reread Ovid,' said Jeremy, 'or consulted the *Oxford Companion to Classical Literature*.'

'Neither is available on my island,' said Julian James, 'as I keep no library there. But you will be able to gather all the essential information in the matter. You must clearly understand, however, that since the island (such as it is) was part of the Roman Empire, the authorities there favour the Roman version of the tale. As far as they are concerned, it was Philomela that was turned into a nightingale, whereupon they saw to it that she was given back her tongue.'

'They?' said Jeremy. 'The authorities?'

'You will soon see for yourselves. Keep your eyes to the north, and when you see twin Romanesque towers rising from the sea, you will know that we are approaching Philomela.'

Len's plan, approved by Provost Helmutt, for killing the Corrington demonstration, was very simple. Cora herself had been whisked away to Egypt, having first arranged, at Len's request, that her rooms should be open to the demonstrators as base HQ and rallying point, as previously determined. She had requested a young sociologist, a certain Bert Beat, to spread the word among the disaffected that her set would still be available despite her own (unavoidable) absence, and she had also asked him to act as host in her stead. All this having been arranged, Len then made the crowning arrangement: some thirty minutes before the commencement of the Provost's Induction, by which time most of the demonstrators would be in Cora's rooms hoovering up her refreshments, the 'Oak' would be closed by the Head Porter and locked from the outside. Since this Oak, or outer door, would itself withstand anything short of a battering ram, and since it had been discreetly reinforced by a camouflaged and brass-bound inner layer by the College Office of Works in the dead of night – since, moreover, the rooms were on the second floor and the windows had been double-glazed and sealed because of Cora's aversion to fresh air – few if any guests would be able to escape until released. The release would take place as soon as the Induction was safely completed, and would be supervised by the Police. Policemen were normally admitted inside Lancaster only at the special request of the Provost, who was in all matters sovereign within the College, and their admittance would normally be ill regarded, except in extreme circumstances, even by the more orderly Dons and Undergraduates. The excuse on this occasion was to be that the heavy use of injurious drugs was suspected.

'There be several of them on the needle or sniffing,' said Len, 'so the tip-off will be perfectly genuine in its kind. The head of the Police anti-drug outfit is an old ally of mine, and it won't be the first time we've had reason to be grateful to one another.'

Marigold was not told about the plan, as it was thought she would regard it as unsporting.

In the event everything went very well. Almost all the demonstrators were firmly locked into Cora's capacious suite at two-thirty p.m. The Procession from the Provost's Lodging to the Chapel was conducted with decorum; and the Provost was induced and sworn to the accompaniment of Prayers and Musick with no dissent other than the vomiting of a bilious quirister. On the way back to the Provost's Lodging (for a Refection of Oysters and Lampreys) the Procession was briefly delayed by two Korean students, who had escaped being mewed up in Cora's set by their unpunctuality and had hung about in order to unfold a banner which proclaimed: FILTHY RACIST HELMUTT IS A STINKING RICH YID.

The banner bearers were quite properly apprehended by four Under Porters, and were subsequently brought before a Race Relations Tribunal which excused their 'Justifiable discrimination'.

The Provost having arrived safely at his Lodging, the Police opened and raided Cora Corrington's set of rooms, where the frustrated demonstrators had been making the best of a bad job. The Police were able to charge twenty-three of these (who had made up a sexual daisy chain) with indecent and in some cases criminal behaviour, nineteen with carrying heroin (two of them enough to be classed as 'pushers'), twelve with carrying cocaine, seventeen with carrying hashish, and four with possessing bags of assorted joy balls variously disguised as fruit pastilles, chocolate truffles and humbugs.

Both Cora's lavatories had been blocked by discarded syringes and knickers.

Depressed by the premature dispersal of what was rapidly becoming the most promising party, the demonstrators (those that were not under arrest) departed sullenly but peacefully. One was left behind and discovered by Cora, on her return from Egypt some weeks later, in a deteriorating condition in a wardrobe. It appeared at the inquest that he had purchased 'smack' mixed with Vim in an unwholesome ratio from an Assistant Reader in the Moral Sciences.

Of those charged, seventeen were Dons or Undergraduates of other Colleges or Universities, eleven were Dons of Lancaster (including Bert Beat), and three were competitors by dissertation for Fellowships of Lancaster or Doctorates of Philosophy. The dead man was also from Lancaster. Anyone else concerned was unconnected with Cambridge or any other University.

'A good haul,' remarked Jacquiz Helmutt, on the evening of his Induction. 'Fourteen of our own worst troublemakers out of the way, for a very long time, I hope. So simple and effective, my dear Len. I wonder it isn't done more often…not so much in Cambridge, where most Colleges other than Lancaster are in fairly good order these days, but in bloody places like Essex and Warwick.'

'There's a simple reason why not, Provost. Nowhere, except in a privileged place like this, would there be a set of rooms big enough for all the revolutionaries to be admitted, or food and drink nice enough to entice them, or, my dear Provost, an outer door strong enough to keep them safely stashed once they were inside. Can you imagine an operation like this being mounted in the Administration box occupied by a Don at Birmingham or even in the Madame Mao Refectory Centre, with cold stale pizza on offer, and a set of gerry-built fire-doors for the students to scuttle out of in all directions?'

'Fire,' said Sir Jacquiz thoughtfully: 'now there's an interesting concept.'

'Come, come, Provost dear,' replied Len, complacently admiring his yellow socks with rainbow clocks and his carnelian stove-pipe trousers: 'we mustn't overreach ourselves, now must we?'

'Eleventh century, these two towers,' said Julian James: 'The Chapter House, in which we shall be spending the night, is a little later. Bustle about, boys, and find the wood for a fire – two fires. We need one on the beach, by the light of which we shall sup; and one in the Chapter House, to keep the creatures of the night away from us as we sleep.'

'The creatures of the night?' said Fielding. 'More vampires?'

'No. Nightingales,' smiled Julian, and disappeared into the sand dunes, which came almost up to the feet of the two towers.

These were joined, rather weirdly, by a tracery screen of delicately carven wood, with curved daggers and mouchettes, fourteenth-century at Fielding's guess. A Rood Screen, thought Fielding; but it could not be that, as the two towers must have been at the extreme West End of the Church of Basilica or whatever of which they were the sole remains. Julian, thought Fielding, had said nothing about the screen, any more than he had explained his bizarre reference (only moments ago) to the nightingales.

The Chapter House was a low, barrel-vaulted chamber, lit (had it not already been dusk) by a row of lancet windows in its south wall, and adjoined and partly canopied by traces of the ruined arcade on which it had once opened and which had been the northern side of a small northern cloister.

'Monks,' said Jeremy arriving with a load of rotting olive wood: 'extraordinary place to find a monastery.'

'Philomela,' Julian said, 'was part of the Roman Empire. No reason why there shouldn't have been an early Romish community here, so out of the way that it survived the depredations of the Goths and the rest, and then, much later, started to build…with stone from the mainland.'

'No reason at all,' said Jeremy, 'as far as all of that goes. What I meant, Fielding, is that there is something quite definitely *wrong* about this island. There are these pleasant sand dunes… which probably go round the coast line of the entire island or islet…and inside these, if you survey the scene carefully…' … which could still just be done, despite the deepening (and totally silent) twilight…

'…there is a meadow, almost flat, but in fact very slightly convex, convex with almost mathematical precision, the highest part being dead in the centre…and the whole evenly scattered with small cypress trees. Except for the area which must have been occupied by the Abbey, and for a small grove of olives to the south, presumably the descendants of the olive trees which the good brothers once cultivated, the whole place, within the circumference of the sand dunes – diameter roughly half a mile – is covered, Fielding, by these cypresses, all of which are pretty well equidistant at ten yards one from the other. There are no irregularities, no bumps or knolls or bowls on the surface of the meadow, no large or dominating trees or groups of trees, no fine Aleppo pines, no cedars, not even a cypress that is taller, however slightly taller, than the rest. Look, Fielding; this whole islet, the central apex of which is perhaps twenty feet higher than sea level, is covered with these equidistant cypresses of small and equal height. There has to be something wrong here.'

'Perhaps that is why the monks came?'

'And why they left?'

'I've built a fire on the beach,' said Julian James' voice behind them. 'You chaps don't seem to have done much about the Chapter House. Luckily there is a store of wood in one corner left over from my last visit.'

'I don't care much for this Chapter House,' said Fielding: 'I'd sooner sleep by the fire on the beach.'

'Me too,' said Jeremy. 'Right out of sight of these horrible cypresses.'

'You seem to have taken against my island,' said Julian lightly: 'Try not to be hostile. The Authorities may not like it.' He lowered his voice. 'For years I have been trying to persuade the Priest to come here. He has powers as an exorcist. Finally he came – about a six-month ago. We landed at noon. He came and stood here, where we are now, and said there was nothing we could do except leave – at all cost leave before dark, even if it meant a night at sea.'

'And now you have brought *us* here…to spend the night?'

'If we are polite, the Authorities will protect us.'

'What authorities? Protect us against what?'

'Against the nightingales that come from the trees.'

'*From those cypresses*, for Christ's sake? Anyway, *what* authorities?'

'Come,' said Julian: 'on the beach is a fire ready to be lit. Not far from it is a small cove of rock, the only rock on the entire coast of the island, and just inside it is a trap which the monks made, to catch crayfish and lobsters. We shall eat fresh grilled lobster, and you shall hear the truth of this island, and know why I have brought you here.'

His weekend of 'Petty Absit' from School brought Marius to Carmilla's set in Lancaster. Somewhat to Marius' annoyance,

Balbo Blakeney was hanging about the place, talking about a demonstration that had been staged, or rather, Marius gathered, not been staged, against the new Provost. It appeared that many people, among them several Fellows of Lancaster, had been arrested by the Police because they had been taking part in a public orgy, and quite a few more had been charged with possession of large quantities of heavy drugs. The latter had been held in custody, the former released on bail.

'I wonder,' said Balbo, 'to what extent our orgiasts were medically examined before being let out.'

'Does it really matter, darling?' said Carmilla, who had a very soft spot for Balbo.

'It will do soon,' said Balbo darkly. 'As you know, my official position here is Steward of Wines and Comestibles. As you also know, I was once quite well known as a biochemist. I have kept up some of my connections, and I find that there is very curious news from America. A new venereal disease, largely but not entirely transmitted from one bugger to another.'

'I had heard something about it, Balbo. Thank God no one had it in the Middle Ages,' said Carmilla, who specialized in mediaeval diseases: 'There are quite enough complications from eleven to fifteen hundred without a Buggers' Pest to add to them. But what has this to do with those arrests the other day?'

'If the Police had conducted a careful medical examination of those arrested,' said Balbo, 'though mind you it would have had to be a very thorough and well informed one, they might have discovered that some of our revellers were infected with this new business. Some of them are known to be buggers, some of them were actually buggering when the Police arrived – and most of them spend a lot of time in America, or minding other people's business in black African States. Now, the news of this disease may have come from America, but the disease itself could well have come from Africa. It is, in any case at all, rife among African negroes.'

'Black men,' emended Carmilla.

'Niggers,' re-emended Balbo.

'So you think…that some quite senior men in this College… might have this new disease of yours?'

'Not mine,' said Balbo, 'or not yet. But who knows what might happen if these people go round distributing the bug into wash-basins and lavatory bowls? I'm off to Grantchester to have a good talk to the Provost about it. Marigold may take notice even if he doesn't.'

'Oh dear,' said Carmilla, soon after Balbo had left, 'how off-putting it is, all that kind of talk.'

'It hasn't put me off,' said Marius: 'Look.'

'Green eyes,' said Carmilla.

'I love the way you feel me. It's just like my mother used to, when I was little. In those days I wasn't yet circumcised. "Let's just see," my mother used to say, "how my big boy's getting on." And then, when I went as hard as a conker but my foreskin wouldn't slide back, "Perhaps we ought to ask a doctor." But she never did. She just continued her own investigations from time to time. Once she taught me the trick, I hardly ever stopped playing with myself.'

'Show me.'

'You show me too.'

'Oh dear,' said Carmilla, 'this is rather infantile.'

'What does it matter if it is,' said Marius, 'so long as we enjoy it.'

When Balbo Blakeney arrived in Sir Jacquiz Helmutt's riverside house at Grantchester in order to warn the Provost and his wife about the new disease, he found them both inattentive. Marigold, it seemed, had had some kind of communication about the twins, while Sir Jacquiz was gloating over an unofficial Police report on those Fellows of the College that had been charged with possession of dangerous drugs.

'*Not* just pot,' Sir Jacquiz said; 'Oh dear me, no. Tons of everything else. Seven of our nastiest men, Balbo, are going to be put away for ages and ages. Highly comical. For years they have felt safe in this College, knowing that the Police could not enter without the Provost's permission, which was never given. Then they help to create a situation in which I am fully justified in summoning the Police, indeed have no alternative, and they are caught out, just like that, the victims of their own mindless presumption.'

'A very serious question arises, Provost,' said Balbo Blakeney, 'about this new disease which others of our sodality may be importing from America or Africa. The danger of infection – '

' – Is absolutely nil unless one plays naughty games with such people oneself,' said Marigold, whose information in the field was non-scientific but far more up to date. 'Don't fetch out *that* bogey, Balbo,' she said as she went back to her letter.

'Of course,' said Jacquiz, 'there are still a lot of very annoying Fellows left, quite apart from those that are going to be sentenced for drug offences or those who, one hopes, will soon die of this helpful new American disease. Or did you say it was African?'

'Those that are left will mind their p's and q's,' said Balbo, who had decided to take a new line on the matter as his friends clearly found his first one tedious. 'You see, all these free trips and conferences of theirs, which they enjoy so much, are contingent on their belonging to a peaceable College of sound repute. However frenzied the Causes or potty the Institutions which send our colleagues round the world in luxury and licence, such Causes and Institutions (simply because they are so ludicrous) need and much prefer to engage, for propaganda purposes, men who come from a supposedly responsible background and therefore savour of sanity. Now, this pigs' breakfast in Cora's rooms will have done the College a lot of harm on the quango and quackery markets, Provost, and those that have not been caught out are going to behave like little angels in order to ensure that Lancaster recovers its balance as quickly as possible and is once again considered a suitable source of *conferenciers* and freeloaders. Your reign will commence with a golden *quinquennium* of tranquillity.'

'How boring you make it sound,' said Marigold. 'Now tell me, you two: what am I to make of this letter from Earle Restarick about the twins? He writes that he has arranged for them to attend the new University of Patras in the North West Peloponnese, where they are to read Ancient Greek and Archaeology. I think they will enjoy that, but surely they will have to talk to people more than they've been used to. I don't think they will enjoy *that*.'

'Marigold,' said Jacquiz gently, 'you know perfectly well that this letter of Earle's, and all that will succeed it, is just a fiction to help us explain, in case of enquiry, where the twins have gone to and why.'

'Suppose,' said Balbo, 'that the authorities *did* enquire, and you showed them that letter, and then suppose they actually wrote to Patras to pursue the matter?'

'I should send an emergency message to Earle Restarick the minute that anyone questioned me, warning him to intercept any letter to Patras, which he could easily do, and forge a suitable one back. For good measure, he would very soon switch the seat of the twins' education.'

'Such a pity,' said Marigold, 'to move them, just as they're settled in Patras. A very pleasant town, I remember.'

'Marigold,' said Helmutt, 'the twins are not settled in Patras. This letter, as you very well know, is just made up by Restarick in case there should be trouble.'

'I can't help thinking of them at Patras. Walking along the Arcades. Going down to the shore of the Gulf of Corinth to swim – remember how they loved swimming? Happily studying Archaeology. It would be so nice for them.'

'Nice but not true. Nobody knows where the twins are. If they want us to know, they will let us, in their own good time.'

'They have so long before them,' sighed Marigold: 'They might forget about us, until it was too late.'

October rain dashed at the window. A yellow willow drooped by the river.

'I think,' said Jacquiz patiently, 'that you should not wonder about them any more.'

'Suppose,' said Balbo, who was fond of hypotheses; 'that they *did* appear to this chap, Restarick, and he wrote to you about it. How would you know that this wasn't just fiction, like the rest of his letters?'

'In the case of their really turning up,' said Jacquiz, 'there is an agreed code word with which Restarick will preface his account. "From the Ebony Gate", he will write. The Ebony Gate, as you of all people will recall, Balbo, is the gate through which the true dreams come up from Styx to mankind.'

As the fire died and the moon swung over the beach of Philomela, Julian James said, 'The monks came from Lecce. They were of the very early order *Auctoritatis Agni*, that is, of the Authority or Power of the Lamb. Hence the title of the "Authorities", often applied to them in respect – or in irony.

'Now let me tell you about this island, to which the monks first came in about 400 AD. The first we hear of it is from the learned Greek Geographer, Tinios of Alexandria. It was originally the property, he tells us, of the Macedonian witch, Thestylis, who had it as a gift from Zeus (in return for services rendered) after the deposition of Cronos. A millennium or two after that, the Thracian Queen Procne was sent to join her there. Procne, as we were saying this afternoon, had been changed into a nightingale. Later, she had been exiled from her own country of Thrace, partly because she was held as abominable for her butchery of her own child, and partly because the inhabitants were becoming very bored indeed with her nocturnal reiterations of guilt and penitence. So the Thracian enchantress, Olympias, who, as Alexander's mother had more than enough troubles of her own to cope with, banished Procne to the island of her sister-enchantress, Thestylis, who agreed that the bird should be allowed to live there and sing her painful nightly ditties, on condition that she acted as a lookout for Thestylis, spending all her days in flying round the island and giving Thestylis *cave* if she spotted anything approaching over the sea.

'Now, about 700 years later, in 395 AD, it so happened that the Order of the Authorities in Lecce fell foul of the ecclesiastical establishment because of their leanings towards some Gnostic heresy which proposed a Dual or split God, half good and half evil. They were sentenced to be burnt; most were, but some escaped in a ship and came to Thestylis and Procne's island, where the sailors, though they had been paid in advance to ferry the monks to Antioch, put them ashore.'

'And whose story is this?' enquired Fielding. 'It can hardly be Tinios of Alexandria still talking.'

'The story is told in the records kept by the monks themselves.'

'I look forward to seeing a copy.'

'When Procne had warned Thestylis of the approach of the shipload of monks,' said Julian James, ignoring Fielding's cavalier request, 'Thestylis had made ready, in the manner of a minor Circe, to transform into beasts any men that landed; but the monks' partial belief in a God of Evil saved them, and all contrived to live amicably together. The monks, being from Italy, required Procne, as a nightingale, to assume the Latin name for nightingale, "Philomela"; and Thestylis required an annual bout of fornication with all the monks, one after the other, from which she gave birth, twelve months later, to a crop of five males and five females (and was instantly re-impregnated). The female infants were strangled in case they should grow into rivals to Thestylis, and the males were brought up to become monks at puberty, when they would join the queue at the annual fecundation of Thestylis. All of which worked beautifully for several centuries. The monks rutted yearly with the witch, such an exhausting business that it was a year before they were again capable of tumescence; Thestylis yearly produced enough infant monks to keep the thing going; Philomela, as she was now called, flew round and round the island all day to protect it and gradually developed a more varied repertoire of songs by night, to everyone's relief.

'Then two things happened. Philomela acquired a mate (who was carried over by a storm from Epirus) and started to lay eggs; and Thestylis (by now several thousand years old though comely as ever) died in childbirth. The oldest monk – the Abbot – claimed kingship over the island as Thestylis' senior male heir; but Philomela disputed the inheritance, saying that for years before the monks came she and Thestylis had been joint rulers of the island and now the kingdom must be hers. When the monks disputed this, Philomela and her mate ordered their progeny to peck out the monks' eyes. A truce was eventually agreed. The monks would build an Abbey Church and a Cloister, and these, with their olive grove, should be their domain held on vassalage to Philomela, who was now undisputed Queen of the Island and Realm of Philomela, as it would henceforth be called.'

'When did the cypresses come?' said Fielding.

'They were always here.'

'I cannot think that the place was worth quarrelling about.'

'You should not say that in the presence of those that have spent centuries in the quarrel.'

Fielding shrugged. A nightingale began to sing from the centre of the cypresses: others joined it, and yet others.

'I always thought they sang singly,' Jeremy said.

'Not here – or not since Philomela mated and began to have children. Our history has now come to the beginning of the eleventh century. The monks built the Church and the Cloister – '

' – Who instructed them,' said Fielding, 'in the Romanesque style? No one had left the island or come to it since the Order *Auctoritasis Agni* arrived at the end of the Fourth Century AD, except for the Nightingale's Mate.'

'The architect was a monk inspired by one or other of his two Gods,' said Julian.

'And the stone?'

'Miraculously transported. Now then. After the Authorities had built their new Monastery, things went on well enough for another four centuries or so, for although their number was no longer renewed by Thestylis' annual parturition, many of them had inherited her powers of longevity. So they had much to be thankful for. But suddenly they had a collective fit of megalomania and decided that, having lived there so long, they were the rightful lords of the island after all. The nightingales, they said, were only birds. Whereupon they were attacked by the nightingales (whose number was now many myriads) with sustained ferocity, and fended them off only by invoking the spirit of Thestylis (being her children in need) and raising her from the dead. Already the nightingales had pecked away the fabric of the Church – '

' – Do you really,' said Fielding, 'expect us to believe any of this?'

'You'll know what to believe – and believe it you will because there is evidence – quite soon enough. Now hear me out,' said Julian James. 'Already the nightingales had destroyed the fabric of the Church, which was loosely scattered or buried in its precinct, leaving only the two West Towers. Thestylis put a benignant spell on these, preventing their destruction, and joined them together by a double screen (yes, double) of beautiful tracery, enabling the monks (her sons) to take shelter in the narrow space between the two screens. Thestylis was then abruptly recalled to Cocytus…while the monks, some fifty of them, huddled between the screens, their only defence from the now implacable nightingales, who took the opportunity to destroy most of the Cloister as well. Because of their huge numbers, and the discipline and organization enforced by their Father and Mother, they had no problems in dismantling the masonry – except in the case of the Two Towers and the screen, which were protected by Thestylis' spell. Finally, when all the monks save the Abbot and three of the Council were dead of starvation, a treaty was made. The Abbot would absolutely and forever recognize Philomela's rule over her eponymous islet, provided the siege of the mewed and now rotting monks was lifted. This was done. The four surviving authorities, last of their Order and having not even a resurrected Thestylis to conceive more, dragged out their days between the Chapter House and the beach, at last withdrew into the screen to die, and extracted a promise from the nightingales that their bodies would be respected and no effort made, then or ever, to magick away Thestylis' spell and undemine the towers or the screen. And there, from that day to this, the four last of the Authorities have sat enthroned in a row, ready to invoke Philomela's promise if the nightingales show any signs of interfering with what is left in the precinct.'

'Yet we need a fire in the Chapter House,' said Jeremy, 'to protect us against these nightingales?'

'They do not like strangers. But if there is a fire by the light of which the Four Authorities can watch us sleeping, the nightingales will respect Philomela's promise to the Abbot and not infest other members of the human, the Authorities', race.'

The immense chorus of nightingales wailed over the islet, nearly deafening the party on the beach.

'How did the island come to belong to your family?' asked Jeremy.

'By conquest. Many years after the last of the Authorities died within the screen, a pirate ancestor of mine, sailing from Corfu, discovered the place and disembarked on to it. The hostility of the birds was plain, but provided the visiting pirates kept to the beach and the area of the Olive Grove and the Monastery, they were left unmolested.'

'Look,' said Jeremy: 'all this about Thestylis and her brood of dualist monks has to be nonsense. There are two realities here. Those birds singing; and those horrible cypress trees, in which, one must suppose, the nightingales somehow contrive to live. Explain those and I'll sleep easy.'

Julian James chuckled, not very amiably.

'I'll explain absolutely everything here,' he said, 'as I told you I would – producing the evidence. First of all, mere Follies: fake Romanesque towers, a fake fourteenth-century screen, fake remains of a cloister. As for the nightingales, they are a recorded and much amplified sound effect. The trees were carefully selected and planted by myself, most of them taken from my estate on Corfu.'

'Why, Julian?'

'To amuse myself. I have had little to do since I came to Greece. I wanted to see…if could take people in.'

'An expensive amusement?'

'My family was rich, if not as rich as yours, Jeremy. No price too high for a good joke, as you know very well for yourself. And I did take people in. I took the Priest in. I have just taken you in.'

'Not with that absurd legend.'

'Perhaps not. But you were worried by other things. And with good reason, Jeremy and Fielding. For now we come to the cream of the joke: to the reality and to the evidence. One thing I told you is true. That screen is indeed a hollow one, despite its appearance. I had great fun with the architectural spooling; but I also had other purposes. Come and see.'

Julian dragged a brand from the fire and lit them all through the dunes. He put out a hand to the screen that now faced them. A door opened inwards. By the light of the brand Fielding and Jeremy could see a second screen about four feet apart from the nearer one. The ground between the two was thickly littered with bones.

'I keep the skulls at home in Agios Andreas to drink out of,' said Julian. 'Some, having heard and partly believed the legend, died from the prolonged torment of the Nightingales' song; others from fear of the ever watchful trees, which they began to suppose were creeping towards them – though when they looked they were always back in their right place. A few of the stronger minded lingered too long for convenience and had to be assisted to their quietus. In all cases the bones stay here and the heads return to Corfu.'

'Julian...'

'Don't worry, Fielding. This is not for you, my old friend and commander, nor for your friend. It happens when I bring those whom I hate.'

'Whom do you hate?'

'Those that insult Greece and disgrace England by coming and *strutting* in Corfu. Whether noble or gentle or common, it is those that strut whom I hate; and when I see them I try to lure them here, on the pretence of an outing, and leave them... to the Nightingales and the cypresses – this evil which I have made and which so appalled the Priest.'

'Surely,' said Jeremy coolly, 'such people are eventually missed?'

'Oh yes. Eventually.'

'And their disappearance attributed to yourself?'

'The Police, as I have told you, do not care to come to Agio Andreas, except for important affairs such as politics. The people of the island do not much mind what becomes of foreigners that *strut* among them. Come to that, other foreigners do not mind what becomes of them either. The boat sets out at night – on a private and exclusive "Mystery Tour" – and no one sees it leaving except the fishermen of Agios Andreas, who have politely guided the tourists (never more than two or three of them, you understand) down to my quay. No one, except my fishermen, sees where or how or whither the tourists have departed, and certainly nobody cares. For there are so few of them, as I say, and those few not very pleasant people…the strutters. Accidents and disappearances do happen. Why worry? Either they will turn up again, people think; or they will not – and the world none the poorer if they don't. There is, in any case, no explanation.'

'Sooner or later there will be busybodies, who will make enquiries for the sheer love of interference and drawing attention to themselves.'

'You are probably right,' said Julian. 'Then my game will be over. But meanwhile, so long as I am not greedy, I may continue to dispose of this scum for perhaps quite a long time. Unless, of course, you two should care to betray me.'

'To whom?' said Fielding. 'I have no time nor taste for lengthy processes of delation in foreign parts.'

'And you, Jeremy Morrison?'

'I have a journey to make.'

'Well, then,' said Julian. 'It is, after all, a pretty harmless hobby, removing strutters from the world.'

'Positively beneficial,' said Jeremy, 'from almost any point of view.'

'And so to bed,' said Julian. He peered through the dunes at the Two-eyed No Name, which rode at anchor some twenty yards out. 'One of you might just as well sleep on board. The other should come with me to the "Chapter House". As you now know, the Nightingales will not attack you if you stay on the beach – but the fleas will.'

Piero Caspar invited 'Greco' Barraclough, along with his attendant 'squire', Nicos Pandouros, and also Len the Provost's Private Secretary, to spend a night at his house in the Fens, the one which he had inherited from Ptolemaeos Tunne.

'Carmilla is not looking well,' said Piero, 'after her visit from Marius Stern.'

They were sitting in the kitchen eating fenland delicacies prepared for them by Piero's cook, Jerome Adorer of Johannes the Prophet Scourge of Asmodai Smith. In Ptolemaeos' time two women called Mrs Gurt and Mrs Statch had been employed, but since they were filthy, drunk, venomous and dishonest, and also fancied themselves as witches (not altogether without reason), Piero had dismissed them, with a liberal gratuity to arrest their malice, soon after Ptolemaeos' death. Jerome Adorer of Johannes was a far better cook (his Fenland Water Slugs in Saffron from Saffron Walden were quite memorable), and he was also deaf and dumb, which meant, as Piero remarked, that he could play the democrat by letting Jerome sit with himself and his guests at meals (in the intervals of serving, of course) without suffering the risk of being detected in indiscretion or the tedium of having to listen to lower-class drivel or grievance.

And now, as Jerome finished helping Piero to Quy Eels baked in Hip Syrup and then sat down to shovel the remaining eels (about two-thirds) out of the dish and into his own parabolic mouth, Piero went on: 'Normally she looks splendid after a day or two with that green-eyed Cupid. This time she looks ghastly. Eyes like piss-holes in grimy, melting slush. What can have happened? It can't just be that the fornication and the rest have gone wrong. That little brute must have upset her some other way. Or be putting pressure on her. Or be causing grave worry of some kind. Any suggestions?'

'Carmilla and Theodosia are always bothering,' said Len, 'about the influence over Marius of a master at his School called Raisley Conyngham. Perhaps that influence was evident this last weekend?'

'In what connection "evident"?' said Barraclough. 'How strongly and in what way?'

'Why do you not simply ask Carmilla?' said Nicos. 'Len, at least, knows her well enough to do so.'

'I have asked her,' said Len. 'She don't answer. Just sighs like a furnace and shakes her head.'

'She is not normally reticent,' said Piero. 'Why so now?'

'Perhaps she is guilty,' said Barraclough, 'that she, a woman of comparative maturity, should be trifling and pleasuring with a little boy?'

'Not so little,' said Nicos.

'Too little for her.'

'Perhaps he is demanding something of her,' said Len.

'Not money,' said Piero: 'He has plenty.'

'Love?' said Nicos. 'Perhaps he is demanding too much love?'

'I don't think,' said Piero, 'that Marius cares all that about love. I think Carmilla is worried, is distressed, because Marius does not ask for enough of her love.'

'Righty,' said Len. 'It is always possible that the love he wants is really Raisley Conyngham's. This is what Conyngham's young henchman, Milo Hedley, implied, when he was staying in the Lodging last summer. He evidently wasn't meant to be talking about Marius in the house of Marius' grandfather, but I managed to take him by surprise. I pressed him with wine and tricked him – clever old me – by asking some question about that very peculiar stampede of racehorses, in which Conyngham was somehow involved, at Belhampton last spring. Milo had had a goodish whack at the Taylor 'forty-seven and was eager to show that he was in the know about that lark and about a great deal more. "The whole thing was got up round Marius," said Milo; "it was to make Marius understand that, like God, Raisley giveth and Raisley taketh away; that Raisley comforteth in all afflictions and brings honey and handmaidens to the sore oppressed. Not really necessary, I think. Unlike that little girl Tessa (who took off at the first whiff of brimstone) Marius was hooked on Raisley from the start. He needed no spells to bind him closer, no powders or nostrums to addict him. He had an *animan naturaliter Raisleyanam* – he was Raisley's boy from the word go." '

'Why?' said Piero.

'Yes, yes, why, why?' echoed Nicos and Barraclough.

'Have you ever seen a picture,' said Len, 'a picture by Caravaggio, known as "The Calling of Matthew".'

'Matthew is gambling with his squalid cronies,' said Nero. 'Christ has just joined the kibbitzers, and points his arm (rather limply) across the table at Matthew?'

'That's the one,' said Len; 'in the Church of San Luigi dei Francesi in Rome. As soon as Matthew sees Christ, he lowers his head, in truculent assent. He knows that Christ is his destiny forever, will he, nill he. It must have been rather the same, I think, with Marius. As soon as he saw Conyngham, he knew that he was for him and for none other. He did not even pause, like Matthew, to be truculent or resentful at having his life interfered with. And yet he had better cause to be bitter than Matthew. Matthew was being called from a life of piggery and greed to follow the Master; Marius was being called from a life of kindness and decency to serve Beelzebub…Why was the call so powerful, you ask? Well, as the Lord has compulsive attraction for those that possess, as Matthew did, an inkling of goodness, so Satan has a similar, and fateful, attraction for those who, like Marius, harbour a patch of darkness. If no Christ or no Raisley turns up, then the goodness or the darkness probably stays unprobed, unsuspected. But as it was, Raisley came to call to and call up the evil in Marius, and from that moment it began to bubble and simmer, much as the awakened virtue must have frothed in the veins of Matthew – the same kind of chemistry but, oh, how different the two catalysts that stirred the molecules.'

'And how does this diagnosis help us to help Carmilla?'

'Oh, it doesn't,' said Len. 'Carmilla knew the sort of thing she was taking on, no one better. So now the poor darling must shift for herself as best she can.'

Isobel Stern stood Oenone Guiscard a purple ice-cream in the Bar of the General Store (*Alimentations*) of St-Bertrand-de-Comminges. This was uncharacteristic, as Isobel, these days, was as tight as her own arsehole, as her friend Jo-Jo Guiscard, Oenone's mother, used to put it. It was possible that Isobel paid for the ice-cream because she was very fond of Oenone. In any event, Jo-Jo had had to pay for her own Pernod, and was now sulking over it.

'Radigund's won't take Oenone till she's thirteen,' she said. She tore up the letter which she had just collected from the *Poste Restante* along the street and threw it on the floor. Oenone picked up the bits.

'Naughty mama,' she said, and took them over to a litter basket.

'I told you Radigund's wouldn't look at her for years yet,' said Isobel: 'it's the equivalent of a boys' public school.'

'I only wrote to book her a place.'

'Well then?'

'It seems they'll want to interview her when she's ten and examine her when she's twelve,' said Jo-Jo. 'That's what made me so cross. How will she ever pass an exam into an English school like Radigund's if we go on living in a place like this?'

'Do you want to live anywhere else?'

'No. I love it here,' said Jo-Jo. 'So does Jean-Marie.'

'And so does Oenone,' Oenone said.

'But you must start being educated,' said her mother.

'When Rosie comes at Christmas,' said Isobel, 'she can start teaching Oenone to read, write and number. I shall expect you to pay for it, of course.'

'Of course,' said Jo-Jo; 'and I shall pay very well. I shall want Rosie to have her full reward.'

'You can pay the money to me,' said Isobel. 'I'll deduct enough for Rosie's keep, plus ten per cent of the gross for arranging it all, and give the balance to her – after deducting another ten per cent for her share of the electricity bill while she's with us.'

'Christ, you are getting scheenie,' Jo-Jo said. 'I used to find it funny, but I now think it's a disease.'

Isobel looked upset.

'I'm only trying to do what is right and what is for the best,' she said, 'in order to teach my children that money must be earned and taken seriously, not just used like water from a tap.'

'When did you ever earn any money?' Jo-Jo said.

'The fact that I was shamefully brought up does not mean that my children should be,' said Isobel.

'Look, angel-pie,' said Jo-Jo: 'Marius has his own inalienable allowance until he's eighteen; then he gets a very tidy jackpot. Rosie *was* under your control, but that changed after her last birthday, as the lawyer reminded you at the time. Her allowance is smaller than Marius' and so is her jackpot, because your deceased hubby was a rotten old sexist, but they are still (a) inalienable, like Marius', and (b) very substantial, so you must quite simply write her off as any sort of prospect for financial discipline or reform. That boat has left the port, forever.'

'You can't be sure. I've given up with Marius, but it's still possible that Rosie may be amenable.'

"No, it fucking well isn't,' Jo-Jo said. 'Just the other day she telephoned me and said she'd buy a ticket to come over for her "Petty Absit", as she called it – if I thought this was a good idea.'

'She should have telephoned me, her mother.'

'She didn't want a lecture on privilege or egalitarianism. She just wanted to know if we would like to see her and what sort of a mood you was in. I said that you were no worse than usual (although reading Engels was wearing you out), but the trouble was we were all going to Sête for the weekend of her Petty Absit thing to follow up some notion of Jean-Marie's about the Cathars. So she said, fine, she'd fly to Montpellier and meet us at Sête.'

'She said *what*? Such wicked and wasteful ideas she's getting.'

'People do,' said Jo-Jo, 'when they've got their own money. It's called being independent. I told her that such "extravagance" would annoy you, but by all means to risk it. Then you said that a weekend at Sête was too expensive for you, and please to leave Oenone to keep you company and anyway hotels were no place for children…so that's what we did, and found Rosie waiting for us, having cakes and coffee.'

'DECEITFUL,' thundered Isobel. 'If I'd known you were meeting Rosie – '

' – You'd have been even bloodier than you were being, whether you came with us or not. If you'd come you'd have savaged Rosie, and if you hadn't you'd have savaged yourself for missing her. Can't you see, sweetie? This meanness, this horrible carping Socialism, is tearing you into strips. For Christ's sake enjoy what God has given you and stop tormenting yourself and your friends, and making our lives a bloody misery.'

'Auntie Isobel is always very kind to Oenone,' said Oenone, taking Auntie Isobel's hand and covering it with a sticky purple syrup from the vestiges of the ice-cream.

'Thank you, darling,' said Isobel. 'I can't help it, Jo-Jo. I feel what I feel. I cannot spend a luxurious weekend in a hotel at Sête when I know that tramps are drinking metholated spirits and sleeping under newspapers in the streets of London and Paris.'

'But the point is,' said Jo-Jo, 'that knowing this you still hang on to your money. Go and give it all to the tramps, give it all to Oxfam or whatever do-gooding circus you please. But don't just squat on it like a spider *and* torture yourself for having it.'

'If I could make Marius and Rosie give up theirs,' said Isobel, her face suddenly knotting, 'I'd give up mine. But how am I to do that, when Rosie takes weekend trips to Sête, on mere impulse, and is encouraged by my best-loved friend?'

When they reached Dubrovnik, Julian James dined with Fielding and Jeremy in a fish restaurant, paid the bill, then rose and said farewell.

'How shall you get home?' said Fielding.

'I told you. I shall walk.'

'It will take you a long time,' said Jeremy.

'I told you,' said Julian: 'I have all the time in the world.'

When they returned to School after the Petty Absit, Rosie and Tessa arranged to meet Jakki and Carolyn Blessington the following Sunday and walk out to Hurtmore Farm for tea.

'Daddy used to do this with Fielding Gray and Lord Luffham,' said Carolyn, 'forty years ago. During that thing they call THE WAR. It seems that there was very little to eat during THE WAR but the people at Hurtmore Farm somehow went on making delicious cakes.'

'Caroline thinks too much about food,' Rosie said.

'Caro*lyn*,' said Carolyn. 'Haven't you noticed? I changed it some time ago. I thought it would be smarter when I arrived here at School.'

'Daddy is very hurt,' said Jakki: 'he only found out during Petty Absit. He took us racing at Belhampton and backed a horse called Sweet Caroline. He told Carolyn she could have half his winnings as he'd backed it for her. When she explained that she was now called Carolyn, he was very upset. The horse won at thirty-three to one – eighty to one on the Tote – and Daddy got more than four hundred pounds. He told Carolyn she could have it all, if only she'd call herself Caroline again. But of course she wouldn't.'

'He always gives us plenty anyhow,' Carolyn explained, 'now that he has it.'

At tea there was more talk of the Petty Absit. Tessa, as they all knew, had been with the Marchioness Canteloupe, and they were a little shy of asking her about that. So Rosie told them about Sête instead.

'Ancient *Setius*,' Rosie said. 'Very important port. A lovely canal goes through the centre, and our hotel was right on it. There was a large interior atrium with four tiers of bedrooms round it and a glass roof. You got to your bedroom along a balcony which looked down on to the court below. Ever so many people commit suicide.'

'They shouldn't allow balconies like that in a caring society,' said Jakki, grinning all over her face.

'The French could never be a caring society,' said Rosie; 'they're far too sensible. They think that if people want to kill themselves, they should be encouraged to get on with it. "Thou shalt not kill, but needst not strive/Officiously to keep alive." Arthur Hugh Clough, Matthew Arnold's friend.'

'He didn't mean it literally,' said Tessa, who was thinking of Theodosia's lovely long strong legs, and the way in which they slowly parted when she was just going to come, to emit what was almost a male ejaculation (or so Tessa supposed, never having seen a male ejaculation). 'He meant to satirize the worldly attitudes of pitiless privileged people.'

'You're beginning to sound like my mother,' Rosie said. 'Which reminds me: I haven't seen Marius since I got back. Has anyone else?'

'He's in the San,' said Jakki. 'I met him as he was walking over there, all wrapped up like the depths of winter. He said he had a virus.'

'He might have let me know,' Rosie said, and swallowed a lot of honey straight out of the spoon.

'He was looking rather down,' said Jakki. 'He looked as if he'd just been up to something which hadn't gone at all as he wanted it to. Something important. And something nasty.'

The other three girls lowered their heads. Rosie put down the honey spoon on the table, making a mess.

'I think Marius has a kind of demon,' said Tessa.

'Socrates said we all have,' said Rosie.

'Socrates' demons were often good. Marius' is not,' said Tessa. 'He once blamed me for raising an evil spirit that haunted him. I think he raised it himself...then. Now Raisley Conyngham has raised another.'

'Such an attractive old man,' said Carolyn. 'He makes me go quite wet.'

'I dare say,' said Tessa, thinking of the moist hairs between Theodosia's thighs as they parted: 'Mr Conyngham has a funny effect on people. Luckily there are people to protect Marius. His friend, Carmilla Salinger, at Cambridge, will protect him.'

'*Schalom*,' Rosie said.

'The beauty of it is,' said Raisley Conyngham to Milo Hedley, who was having dinner with him at Wilton's in Jermyn Street, 'that although Carmilla is one of the Save Marius Society, it is precisely through her that he will be lost to them. If he can induce her to bring Jeremy back, as is your wish, then she will have lost him forever; for he will have betrayed her and betrayed Jeremy and absolutely betrayed any love that he feels for either.'

'How's all that getting on?' said Milo. 'What a pity we're too early for the woodcock, sir. But a partridge would be nice.'

'Yes,' agreed Raisley: 'no dud red-legs here. Only grey, your true eating...I think, Milo, that it is going fairly well but that there are difficulties. As indeed we might have expected. Marius came back to School after the Petty Absit looking very peaky, so I sent him off to the Sanatorium and told them to give him a week's rest. He will have a lot of improving and amusing books to read, and the best of food and wine, including fresh caviar from Fortnum.'

'The caviar here is thirty pounds for two ounces*,' said Milo.

* 1981 prices. Simon Raven

'Fortnum's is retail and rather cheaper. Not that it much matters.'

'How did you talk the Dame of the Sanatorium into this, sir?'

'She owes me a great many favours, Milo, of one kind or another. So after a day or two I went over to the Sanatorium to see Marius and get a detailed account of activity at Lancaster during the Petty Absit.

'Marius started by giving me a general report of the state of play in the College. It seems that Jacquiz Helmutt is firmly established. He's got rid of a lot of the left-wingers by calling in the Police – *apparently* as a necessary measure of security, but in fact knowing perfectly well that the Police would arrive in the middle of a dope and sodomy party…and make the appropriate arrests.'

'We heard about that in Trinity,' said Milo, as he delicately carved his partridge: 'It's so long since that Lancaster lot saw a Policeman inside the College that they'd forgotten there were any laws in the land.'

'Now they will have remembered. And those that didn't get into trouble, for whatever reasons, are determined to stay out of it. If Lancaster gets into any worse an odour, the international academic treats will be barred to Lancastrians. So the rorty dons of Lancaster are lurking very quietly in Holy Henry's Shade, and long live good king Helmutt. By way of switching Marius on to Carmilla, I asked him what *her* view was. It seems she's a nice moderate girl who hates disorder and regards revolution as the speciality of failed intellectuals (Conrad took the same view, one recalls) who are not receiving enough attention to satisfy their peevish and puffed up egos. So by all means squash them flat, Miss Carmilla would say, but let's not have the boys in blue round too often, in case it becomes a habit.

'At this stage, my dear Milo, it became clear to me that Marius was postponing, for as long as possible, any discussion of his personal relations with Carmilla. So after a little while longer I taxed him with this. His relations with Carmilla, he said, had never been better: affectionate, highly pleasurable, not necessarily permanent (why should they be?) but not just a thing of the moment either. He seemed, Milo, to be looking forward to an enjoyable affair of roughly a year's duration.

'But still, I insisted, something was surely wrong; I could see it in his face as soon as he returned from Cambridge.

'Well, yes; one thing was wrong. Marius then referred me to the briefing I had given him not long ago, about persuading Carmilla to recall Jeremy and Fielding Gray from the voyage on which she had sent them. I had told him to make her love him, he said, love him so much that she could refuse him nothing. But it was now clear that this simply could not be done. Carmilla was a jolly, sensual, loving, loyal, decent, intelligent girl: a grand girl: but she was never going to fall deeply in love, never meant to, did not wish to – was altogether too conscious of the plenteous variety provided by God to tie herself up in monogamous knots. Well, so be it, Marius said: just as well for everyone, perhaps; but where now was he to find a way of compelling or persuading her to bring Jeremy back? Had she been deeply in love with Marius, there would have been no difficulty: she would have done it because he asked or, if necessary, insisted. But as it was she – well – she fonded on him: she would no doubt indulge him in many things: but in cases like this of Jeremy he would have to find a *reason* for requesting her to get him back. And there was no reason. The voyage was a good scheme, it was agreed by all parties, the money had been put up and accepted in good faith, advertisements and declarations had been issued, and contracts signed; there was no reason whatever why Carmilla should order or request Jeremy and Fielding to return, every reason in the world why she shouldn't. So what was Marius to do to keep his promise to me?'

'Difficult. Shall you mind, sir, if I ask for a Welsh Rarebit?'

Raisley ordered two Welsh Rarebit.

'Thank you, sir. And *did* Marius try to keep his promise to you?'

'He did. He told Carmilla a lie. I'd hoped this wouldn't be necessary, for tactical reasons, but it was always on the cards that it would be. Anyway, he did. He said he was very worried about Jeremy. He said that when he met Jeremy at the Provost's Burial in September there had been a kind of desperation about him which he, Marius, had not observed since an occasion, some years before, when Jeremy had come to say goodbye to him at his preparatory school before going on the run. He, Marius, did not, he told Carmilla, care for the notion of a desperate Jeremy let loose in the Mediterranean with the mercurial Fielding Gray as his only guardian.

'In what way "desperate"? Carmilla wanted to know. She was falling for it, Marius says. Her sister, Theodosia, had seen Jeremy (within hours of his visiting Marius) that time just before Jeremy went on the run, and Carmilla had obviously had some account. One reason he was "desperate" in those days was shortage of money: this could not be the case now: so what other ingredient (Carmilla must have been trying to remember) made up the "desperation" which her sister and Marius had observed three years ago and Marius claimed to have observed just the other day.

'In what way "desperate"? Carmilla pressed Marius as they lay in bed on Marius' last afternoon, before he caught the evening train back to School. "Paranoia, for one thing," Marius answered: "thinking he was being violently wronged, and not understood, and that evil report of him was being put about." "He has had a very nasty time of it," Carmilla said: "He is bound to behave oddly at times. That's what we hope to cure by sending him on this journey." Oh, yes, she was falling for Marius' story; but she wasn't buying, not just yet. "Bring him back," Marius said: "He's not safe there, just with Fielding. I know it." '

'Lies, as you say, sir,' said Milo. 'But that he should have told them to his friend, his lover (however temporary), in order to mislead her – this is surely treachery. We have, then, brought him that far.'

'We need the thing to be completed,' said Raisley Conyngham. 'Apart from anything else, *you* want Jeremy back, for your own purposes. And to make this treachery as damnable as we would wish, it must also comprehend Jeremy.'

'It already does. By lying in this way about Jeremy, he has been treacherous to Jeremy.'

'The treachery will not be complete – not twenty-four carat, Milo – until Jeremy is actually brought home by Carmilla's order.'

'And how nearer are we to that?'

'I don't quite know. Neither does Marius. That was what was troubling him. That, and the fact that he has seriously upset Carmilla.'

'That was always going to be necessary.'

'Still, you can't expect him to like doing it.'

'You grow too soft, sir. So does Marius. If he is feeling regret, that may in some sense, in some part, redeem him. We do not want him redeemed.'

'We cannot have everything at once, Milo. He has now told a vicious and treacherous lie, and the thing is perhaps beginning to work…to fester in Carmilla's breast, to cause fear, anxiety, doubt lest the commission which she had given to Jeremy may prove, after all, ill-advised. Do not be too greedy for too much too quick. Now tell me about Trinity.'

This Milo did while they each drank two large glasses of Marc de Champagne; after which they went outside into Jermyn Street, where Raisley Conyngham stepped into the chauffeur-driven Rolls that would take him back to Farncombe and Milo into the chauffeur-driven Mercedes that would take him back to Cambridge, both cars having been hired and paid for by Raisley Conyngham.

Having with some difficulty found harbourage just north of Split, Jeremy and Fielding visited the Museum of Antiquities. Near the entrance was a Garden God with a colossal erection.

'It feels so warm,' said Fielding: 'almost throbbing.'

'Have a care, dear. It might come all over you.'

'Yummy.'

'I think,' said Jeremy, 'that we had better transfer our attention to this Fountain of Neptune. Neptune has been very good to us so far. Not a puff of unwanted wind.'

'No problems now,' said Fielding, 'now that we're past Albania. We just cling to the coast. At the slightest sign of trouble we put into the shore and stay there until complete calm is restored.'

'It seems a bit…unheroic,' Jeremy said.

'Heroism can come later,' said Fielding, 'when we have passed the Pillars of Hercules.'

'I promise you that I shall have found what I am supposed to be looking for well before we reach the Pillars of Hercules.'

'Who's being unheroic now? You know,' said Fielding, examining a lively leopard on a Corinthian drinking bowl, 'we really could have asked Julian to accompany us the whole way. As he said, he has plenty of time.'

'How well do you know Julian James, Fielding?'

'I hadn't set eyes on him since we were soldiers in Germany in the early 'fifties. He'd come to us from Lancaster with a National Service Commission.'

'I have heard you say…in another context…that it was more usual in those days for people to do their National Service first and then go up to the University later.'

'True enough. But quite a few did it the other way round.'

'Often because they hoped that something would happen, while they were up at Oxford or Cambridge, to cancel their liability for National Service?'

'What are you getting at, Jeremy?'

'I'm saying that I'm rather relieved that Julian has left us. I'm saying that there is something highly peculiar about him.'

'By most people's standards, no doubt. Of course all those bones inside the Screens must have been the remains of animals, and all that chat about killing tourists by terror was simply his kind – and ours – of black and snobbish humour. That was why there were no skulls. Animal skulls would have given the joke away. But even so,' said Fielding, 'it was a curious fantasy.'

'It wasn't a fantasy. During the Earth Mother hoax,' said Jeremy, 'I had once or twice to tour stricken areas.'

He paused in front of a stone that bore a Greek inscription. This was translated into several languages, among them English, on an adjacent notice:

O PITIFUL REMNANTS OF MAN
REASSEMBLE THEM WHO CAN

' "Pitiful remnants of man," ' said Jeremy. 'That was what I was seeing on my tours. They were just like those bones on Julian's island of Philomela. In neither case the bones of sheep or oxen or what have you, but those of man, proud man; of *Homo Sapiens*. That's why I asked you how well you knew Julian James.'

'Very well, in the Army.'

'Nearly thirty years ago. What happened then?'

'He was demobilized, like all other National Service officers and men. Then he vanished. Obviously, in the light of what we now know, to Agios Andreas, having either inherited it already or being sure of the inheritance. I think one could live thirty years on Corfu easily enough, given a house by the sea like that and a copious library.'

'One might surely get bored, Fielding, every now and then?'

'One might. If so, being well off, one could go somewhere else for a while.'

'Yes. Like one's own island of Philomela.'

'Also Athens, Rome – England.'

'Precisely. And when in England visit one's old College. Lancaster College, Cambridge. Which Julian did when I was a freshman. We didn't meet then – why should we have? – and so he did not recognize me when he found us in Cassiopi. He knew of my later and public role, as Religious Polemicist, but he did not recognize me as the farouche and (in those days) quite slender undergraduate of Lancaster, who watched him while he walked on the Rear Lawn with Tom Llewyllyn one October morning of 1977…bald and purple then as now, and somehow intriguing the unnoticed onlooker, me, who found out his name from one of the older porters and looked him up in the College register and other books of reference.'

'You can't have discovered anything very dramatic.'

'Not at first. Later on, however, he was recorded as President of the Alexandrians – a Dining Club which he founded and for which he procured Official College recognition. The Club collapsed as soon as he went down. Nobody else – according to a college magazine – wanted to take it on. It had a sinister reputation, you see. After its last banquet, in December 1951, seven of its members were struck by food poisoning, two of them fatally.'

'Was Julian attacked?'

'Yes. He would be, wouldn't he? Now, in those days, so I am told by you and others, people didn't fuss so much about that kind of thing as they do now. Accidents. Mishaps. Blame God, or blame the Devil, but for Christ's sake don't let's have a production. That was the attitude, and a very salutary one. What a pretty statuette: Julian must have looked rather like that when young.'

'He did,' said Fielding.

'So who would have suspected him of having anything deliberate to do with the disaster at his Dining Club's banquet? Who cared about it, anyway? In those days the very sound understanding was that things like that will occasionally happen, and the less said the better. No public hysteria, no proles whining for compensation. Still, none of this was calculated to make The Alexandrians a very popular institution, and, as I say, the Club died… and Julian James left the University and was speedily transformed into Cornet James of the 10th Sabre Squadron of the 49th (Earl Hamilton's) Light Dragoons. For, as you have just reminded me, he had opted to postpone his National Service and now it had caught up with him.

'Only it wasn't quite like that, Fielding. Before Julian came up to Lancaster he had obtained temporary exemption from National Service on grounds of a neurotic horror of firearms – something to do with a nasty accident when he was a little boy. So it looked as if he was all set to evade his National Service altogether. All he had to do on leaving Lancaster was to apply for a renewal of the exemption, on the same grounds and supported by the same Doctor and that, one might have thought, would have been that. But not a bit of it. During his last year at Lancaster, soon after that fatal dinner, he applied to be considered as a candidate for a National Service Commission in the 49th Light Dragoons – and was duly accepted as he had once been out shooting with Canteloupe, or Captain Detterling, as he was then, a well-known officer of the Regiment, who had reported on him in a vague but on balance favourable manner.'

'*Shooting*? And him with his horror of firearms?'

'Quite so, my dear. We conclude that he had obtained his original exemption fraudulently, and could probably have continued in it, but that something that happened while he was at Lancaster changed his mind. Could it be that he had developed a taste for death? That he had experimented with it, to his satisfaction? That he rather enjoyed it, and looked forward to being more frequently and intimately associated with it in the Army?'

'Rather speculative, surely? There wasn't much death around in the British Army of the Rhine.'

But what, he now thought, of those two very sanguinary accidents with a half-track under Julian's command? On the way home from that big autumn manoeuvre – what had they called it? – Apocalypse. Two maintenance corporals killed on succeeding days because the vehicle had accidentally been started while they were underneath it. What a dreadful coincidence, everyone in the Mess had said. Poor Julian. But since the accidents had occurred during what were, in effect, conditions of active service…when everyone was very tired… and there could be no possible suggestion of malice…well, *Res Unius Res Omnium*, the corporals being dead did not count among the *Omnium*, and the less said the better. Call a Field Enquiry and fudge it, then get tasteful Captain Fielding Gray to write two of his famous letters to the widows.

'So,' said Fielding to Jeremy in front of a wild mural mosaic of Medusa, 'you think that Julian has been enlivening a pleasant but uneventful life with the occasional stimulus of violent death.'

'I wouldn't wonder.'

'What do you suppose he did do with the skulls…*if* he really disposed of annoying tourists on Philomela?'

'I suppose he did what he said he did. Removed them from the ossuary (after all, he would not wish to leave screamingly obvious evidence about, unlikely as it was to be discovered) and took them home to Agios Andreas to drink out of in private. Like Byron…who, by the way, would have adored this Ganymede: just a hint of hairs appearing, like that choirboy of his at Cambridge or one of his little cricketing friends at Harrow.'

Three weeks after the Petty Absit came the Armistice Exeat; and Teresa Malcolm went again to Theodosia Canteloupe.

Theodosia, now within three months of her time, was positively globular and needed much rest, during which she liked Tessa to lie beside her, quietly scratching her back or her buttocks. One afternoon Theodosia said:

'A girl has been here asking after you.'

'A girl?'

'A rough stable girl, who is employed by my neighbour Sheringham as Head Travelling Lass. She has a large gap between her top front teeth.'

'Gat-toothed Jenny,' said Tessa, tickling Thea at the top of the crack. 'She was in Raisley Conyngham's stables. She must have left him.'

'Do you wish to see this girl?' said Thea, spikily, and wriggled her rear away from Tessa's fingers.

'I'm sorry, but I must. She was a good friend to Marius and me last spring.'

'Very well,' said Theodosia, relenting enough to bring her bottom within range again. 'I shall arrange a car to take you over to Sheringham's.'

'Come too, Thea. A bit of an outing will do you good.'

'I haven't much to say to stable girls.'

'She would have something to say to you. A lot to say to you…all about Marius.'

But Theodosia did not care to hear what Jenny had to say about Marius; and Tessa spoke to the lass alone under the clock in Sheringham's stable yard.

'I'll make no bloody bones about it,' said Jenny. 'I want to see Marius again. While I was still with Mister Raisley Cunting Conyngham that was forbidden. I am free now.'

'Why did you leave Ullacote?' asked Tessa.

'Like you, ducky, I didn't like the smell. I've got coarser nostrils than yours, so at first it didn't get up them. But eventually the stink of – of – '

' – Wickedness, to use a simple word?'

123

'Yes. If you like. And the misery with it – these smells drove me away.'

'Misery?'

'Jack Lamprey. He's losing his touch. I never thought that would happen. However much Jack drank, and however often he tried to feel me up my quim, I always forgave him because of his hand with horses. But it's going, love. God knows why. Perhaps there is a spirit moving at Ullacote that will drive out anything good. For good there was, and Jack Lamprey training the horses was part of it. But it's seeping away, and so me, I just pissed right off one night, before it was too late. And now I'm free of Ullacote and any promise I made to Conyngham; and I want Marius again. What I wanted to ask you was, how do I find him?'

Tessa marvelled at Jenny's stupidity. She must know, thought Tessa, that Marius attends the school at which Raisley Conyngham teaches, that all she has to do is to write to him there –

' – I know what you're thinking,' said Gat-toothed Jenny. 'You're thinking, this lower class slut is too silly to work out where he's at school and get in touch with him there. Have a heart, love. Of course I know where he's at and where I can come at him. I need you to tell me how, to tell me what time would be convenient, how to ask for him when I arrive – what kind of stuff I should wear – '

' – Jenny. You love Marius and I believe he has marvellous memories of you. Just once he started to tell me about you and him in that ambulance, but then he stopped, I haven't been close to him for years now, so he just stopped and started looking as if he wondered why he had ever begun. But even with the little he'd said, I could tell that this was something – well – magic. So I'll tell you how to meet him. But you must please take a message for me. It's a message I can't give him, even though I'm at the same school myself and see him almost every day.'

'I'll take your message.'

'Very well. Now you don't actually want to go to the School – you might meet Mr Conyngham, apart from anything else. Write to him, and say you'll wait for him at the Duke's Arms Hotel in Farncombe. Sunday will be best.'

'Ah. Reckon he'll be bored of a Sunday?'

'No. Oddly enough there's more going on in that School on Sundays than any other day. But on a Sunday he'll be allowed to get away without difficulty. Say you'll be there at three p.m. You'll find no trouble in booking a room, if you want one, as the School parents all stay at the Lake – but make Marius pay for it, because he's rich. And when he comes to you, Jenny, say this to him: whatever it is that Mr Conyngham is trying to make him do now, he must not do it. And more: he must make himself understand why he must not do it.'

'I'll tell 'um. I just want Marius, Teresa love, his arms, his legs and his prick, but I'll tell 'um what you say, and I'll tell 'um there's something foul moving in on Ullacote, and he must shun both the place and its master.'

'I told you last time I was here,' said Marius to Carmilla: 'Jeremy Morrison is in a state of desperation and not to be trusted at large. Least of all on the high seas.'

Marius had come to Lancaster for the School Armistice Exeat. As soon as he had arrived, he had tackled Carmilla in the matter of Jeremy Morrison's re-call, only to find that she had put the thing out of her mind.

'I thought of it at length and with great anxiety,' Carmilla said. 'I thought of it for hours together after you left here last time, and I decided that, on balance, the best thing to do was to let him get on with the voyage. I had hoped that you would come to see it the same way.'

And so now Marius was telling her that he had not come to see it the same way and was mortified that his previous advice had not been acted on.

'I know his moods, and I have warned you, and now I find you have done nothing,' Marius said.

'I know his moods too. My sister and I have known him much longer than you have.'

'*You* never saw him when he was desperate. I did – that time he ran away three years ago. He is desperate now.'

'Theodosia saw him that time he ran away. Just before. She also saw him the other day, just after old Tom's Burial. I have spoken with her about all this, on the telephone, I grant you, but carefully and at great length, and she is certain that Jeremy is *not* now in the same state as he was when he ran away three years ago, and that he is certainly not desperate.'

'What do I have to do to convince you?' Marius said. He rose and walked to the window that looked down on the South Door of the Chapel.

'I do not understand you, Marius.' Carmilla came and stood beside him. 'You knew what was planned for Jeremy. You made no objection. You *saw* Jeremy, here in this room, and later on at the Provost's Burial. At no stage during any of this did you make any objection whatever. But now, now that Jeremy and Fielding have actually gone, now that they are on their journey and there is every sort of difficulty, moral and practical and contractual and logistical, in interfering with them or bringing them home, *now* you insist that we should do so. For Christ's sake, Marius. For Christ's sake.'

'I only recognized the symptoms in Jeremy retrospectively …after he and Fielding had gone. I thought again of our meetings here, and then I started to compare them with the meeting at my prep school – during a Riding Class it was – just before he ran away three years ago. It was only then, Carmilla, when I made this comparison, that I recognized the same disastrous symptoms.'

'Other people, who knew and loved him, recognized no symptoms.'

'I do not want to quarrel over this, Carmilla. I just want Jeremy back.'

'You can't have him back.'

'Carmilla. You do not understand how important this is to me. I am doing this for love.'

'You're being a conceited little bore.'

'Yes,' said Marius, 'I can see you find all this very tiresome. It is tiresome for me too. All I want is to go through to your bed and lie on it with you, tasting your body. But I have to settle this business of Jeremy first.'

'Let me off, Marius. Stop being so horrible. Fielding Gray will take care of Jeremy. Let the voyage prove Jeremy, as it is meant to do, or finally and fully disgrace him, if so it needs must be. Do not interfere, Marius. Come through to bed.'

'Only when I get your word that you will re-call Jeremy. Immediately.'

'I too can be stubborn. Jeremy has been turned over to the God of Ocean, and the God will exalt or destroy him. So be it.'

'Jeremy will destroy himself. As Jeremy is now, the trial you propose is cruel and unfair to him. He is not fit to undertake it.'

'He thought differently. So did all his friends, and so they still do. All his friends except you.'

'And I say this, Carmilla: if you do not bring Jeremy back, as I have requested, I shall make a full public report of the fraud which Canteloupe and your sister are trying to practise on the world in the matter of the inheritance. I shall admit to conniving with Theodosia to beget her child and pass it off as her husband's. I do not think they will punish me – the *naif* and spunky little boy seduced (if not actually molested) by the heartless noblewoman. I *do* think they will punish Canteloupe and Theodosia.'

'And thereby torture me. I know what has got into you, Marius. If I simply submit to this blackmail, the poison will stay in you and rot you, as surely as gangrene or the worm that comes to the dead. There is, in truth, only one hope for you. Come to bed, and I shall tell you what I propose.'

'Is it better with her or with me?' Gat-toothed Jenny said. 'Not that I mind. I'm not the jealous sort. But I'd be glad of a comparison.'

'She...is even more shameless. She does not mind making herself childish or absurd, or even grotesque.'

Marius surveyed Jenny's chunky legs.

'But she does not respond as you do,' said Marius. 'Her responses are disappointingly mild – even when she is at her most abandoned. Curious, that. She *yells* about how she is going to come. Then she just quivers, briefly and elegantly, and it is over. Now you, you rumble and tremble from head to foot. You are volcanic.'

You are also rude-skinned and a bit dirty, he thought. Your toenails are jagged. Your pubic hair is coarse. You have a few extra ones between your breasts. Your hands are certainly kinder than Carmilla's but your fingers have the texture of raw carrots and there are traces of dead eczema on the palms. You rather disgust me, in fact. That first time when Raisley gave you to me in an Ambulance, after the races at Belhampton, that was different because it was dark in the Ambulance, there was a delicious warmth, I could not see you under the blankets, I could only feel you expand and erupt. Now, in the bedside lights (feeble as they are) provided by the Duke's Arms, I can see too much. I shall stay with you just a little longer and then plead an official engagement up at the school. It is Sunday afternoon: I shall say I must have tea with my Housemaster's wife. I hope you won't be hurt, but I must go. You smell. You smelt in the Ambulance, but then so did I that time, because I had shat myself with fright, and although Raisley had cleaned me off there was still a bit of pong on me. There isn't now: there is on you.

'Tessa says,' said Jenny, starting to play with Marius' limp cock, 'that whatever Raisley Conyngham is trying to get you to do, that you must not.'

Damn her. He did not want her to start mussing him about again. But then…her hands were certainly kind. Perhaps he would stay a little longer. Pity her fingers weren't softer, but they were very gentle.

'I am not going to,' said Marius: 'I am going to do something else.'

Something which Raisley will probably approve of almost as much, thought Marius; but at least it is not what he originally commanded. I fear and worship Raisley, I wish him to command me totally: yet it is agreeable to make some slight alteration of one's own. He remembered what Raisley Conyngham had once said about Fate and the Gods in the *Aeneid*: the Gods could not prevent what was willed by Fate from coming about; but they could delay it slightly, interpose minor difficulties, engineer tiny changes. This made them content on the whole; for they had the power to *tinker*. In the same way he, Marius, was made content by having contrived a slight change in that which was willed by the mighty Raisley. True, the contrivance was Carmilla's; but he had brought her to the point of action, had then agreed and connived and compounded with her: he, Marius, like the Gods of Virgil, had played his own part.

His prick was nearly hard now. Yes, he would stay a little.

'Stroke me,' said Jenny: 'stroke my clit.'

Her 'clit'. Could one conceive of Theodosia or Carmilla's talking about their 'clits'?

'So you are promising me,' Jenny said, as he began to oblige her, 'and I shall tell Tessa, if I see her again, that you are not doing what Raisley Conyngham tells you.'

'I am doing what I have decided.'

'Because you know that what he wanted of you was wicked?'

'I am doing what I have decided because it is what I prefer.'

'Is it fair and square?'

'As it happens, yes.'

Though of course it hadn't been at the beginning, the way he'd pressed Carmilla, threatened to peach on the Canteloupes; still it was fair and square now.

'Why can't Tessa talk to me for herself?' he said. 'She sees me every day up at the School.'

'She can't talk to you as long as you are Raisley's. How nice it looks. Do you want to put it in?'

'No. Let's just finish off like this.'

'Don't seem right. All right to start with, but not to finish off with. Wrong, somehow.'

'I'm coming anyway.'

Then,

'I've got to go,' Marius said. 'I'll pay for the room as I leave.' And he went.

'The Empress Theodora,' said Fielding Gray, 'was the most horrible bitch. A talented whore who turned into an Inquisitor. It is the Inquisitor we see here, I think.'

Fielding Gray and Jeremy Morrison looked at the Mosaic of Theodora with her suite in the Chancel of the Church of St Vitalis (San Vitale). She certainly did not resemble a whore, talented or other.

'According to a Greek footnote in Gibbon,' said Jeremy, 'she enjoyed her whoring very much, while it lasted. She used to give exhibitions, you know: she used to put grain and lentils and whatever right into her thing, then lie down and whistle until her pet gander came and started to peck it all out. This threw her – and the audience – into a frenzy.'

'Maisie Malcolm used to give exhibitions like that to special audiences.'

'*Tessa's Aunt*?'

'Tessa's mother, if the truth be told. Tessa was conceived out of whoredom. That's why Maisie goes on posing as her aunt.

One day Tessa might find out…by accident, perhaps…that Maisie was a whore. Now, Maisie wouldn't mind if Teresa found out that her *aunt* had been a whore, but she wouldn't wish her to realize this of her mother. So she remains, before the world and before Tessa, "Auntie Maisie". You know why I'm telling you this?'

'No.'

'Partly because Maisie is always spiteful and unfair about you, and I want you to have a bit of your own back. Partly because I have made an interesting observation which I cannot bear to keep to myself and not get credit for. If you look very carefully at Theodora, you will see that the lineaments of the whore are just detectable, at least by one who knows, under those of the Imperial and Christian Inquisitor. There is just a hint of the affable shopkeeper who deals in her own soiled flesh and offal. It is the same with Maisie. Under the impeccable surface of the respectable hotelier who is the benificent, the almost perfect, aunt, we can occasionally catch a glimpse of the calculating gaiety with which she used to promote and overvalue her carnal conjuring tricks. Very seldom and very briefly she has the air of one who is saying, "And for fifty quid extra I'll coax a Boa Constrictor out of my cunt and then back into it again − for another twenty." Christ, I'm sick of whores, particularly reformed ones. Let's go and see Dante.'

'Dante?'

'His tomb is here in Ravenna. He died in exile from his beloved Florence. As one literary cove to another,' said Fielding Gray, 'I owe him the compliment of a visit. Besides, he would have been interested in you.'

'Oh?' said Jeremy preening a little.

'He had an admiration for con-men and a suppressed envy of them. He did not approve of this indulgence, and in order to redeem himself he awarded con-men disproportionately nasty punishments in his Inferno.'

SIMON RAVEN

'I think,' said Jeremy, 'that Ravenna is a beastly dank hole of a place, and Dante or no Dante I shall be jolly glad to embark again tomorrow. How long will it take us to sail to Brindisi?'

'You are captain of the good ship No Name. You work it out if you want to know. But I thought you told me that we're meant just to drift on and take things as they come.'

'Yes,' said Jeremy. 'But I suppose one must have some sort of a plan. Otherwise we might just drift on forever.'

'Would it matter if we did?'

'You forget. Sooner or later,' said Jeremy, 'I'm supposed to have a revelation.'

'Do you want one?'

'Not all that much, but that's what's in the agreement: revelation. One day I'm meant to come to a place of vision or enlightenment. Like Odysseus.'

'He never came to such a place,' said Fielding. 'He never found the Isles of the Blest (or Blessèd). He just sailed on till he vanished.'

'How do you know?'

'Because if he had found such a place, we should have heard of his finding it. We hear of his desiring it and seeking it, from Tennyson, Kazantzakis and the rest; but we never hear of his finding it. Cavafis was of opinion that the journey was what mattered and that arrival should be delayed as long as possible, indeed forever. True, he was talking of Odysseus' return from Troy, but I'm sure he would have said exactly the same about Odysseus' trip to the West.'

'It's all very well for Cavafis, having these irresponsible fancies. He was a discredited – a disgraced – man.'

'So are you.'

'I'm meant to be rehabilitating and redeeming myself.'

'The journey will see to that. No need to arrive anywhere.'

'That's not what Carmilla and Theodosia think. Anyway, if I never arrive anywhere, nobody will know that I'm redeemed.'

'You will.'

They entered an unremarkable classical erection of the late nineteenth century.

'And here we are *chez* Dante,' said Fielding. 'Why not ask his opinion?'

'What a boring tomb,' said Jeremy.

'That's no way to begin.'

'Downright unattractive.'

'Ask Dante your question.'

'You're his colleague, or so you claim. You ask him for me.'

'All right,' said Fielding. And after a brief pause, 'His answer is that once a man is exiled from his own place, it doesn't much matter whether and when he arrives anywhere else.'

'Perhaps such a man should return to his own place, then.'

'Dante couldn't. They wouldn't have him back in Florence.'

'They might have *me* back in Luffham.'

'Only on sufferance,' said Fielding. 'Not a good solution.'

'Lancaster, then?'

'You don't know enough to be a don.'

'If I paid them enough, they might let me have a set of rooms and just live in the place. Lots of chaps used to do that, without being dons.'

'Not any more. I don't think it's allowed. It smacks of privilege. You have to have some work to do to get let in these days.'

'Backto Farncombe, as a beak?'

'The new Head Man would never have you.'

'Where can I go then?'

'You can drift on round the Mediterranean with me. What we find or do not find is of no consequence at all. Off again tomorrow. We must make sure,' said Fielding Gray, 'that the hotel delivers our laundry to our rooms tonight.'

'Carmilla has guessed that my attempt to persuade her to order Jeremy back was your idea, sir,' said Marius to Raisley Conyngham in the latter's chamber. 'She won't do it. But there is something else she will do. Something she regards as freeing me from your aura and influence. She will let me go to bring back Jeremy myself.'

'She could hardly stop you from doing that if you wished.'

'She could get an injunction against my attempting to make Jeremy break his contract.'

'But as it is, she will leave you a clear field?'

'She will, sir. But she doesn't like the idea of my roving the continent alone, so she will send a guide and tutor with me. Piero Caspar.'

'Why him?'

'She thinks…that he will cleanse me of my evil genius. She regards the whole thing as a test.'

'She's getting mightily keen on tests, she and that sister of hers.'

'She also thinks, sir, that it will take me away from you, and help purge me of you.'

'So you are to be cleansed by Caspar and purged by your search and altogether removed from the area of my influence?'

'Right, sir.'

'God, how silly these women are. If you go with my blessing and a few of my additional instructions, you will remain as much within the area of my influence as ever.'

'That is what I thought you would say, sir. What are your additional instructions?'

'Very broadly, Marius, to *fail* the test Carmilla is really setting you. She thinks that if you find Jeremy, *both* of you are going to be tested. Jeremy's resolve and your sense of decency. She thinks that when you see what this voyage is doing for him – and by the time you find him (she thinks) it will have done a very great deal – you will abandon any further effort to stop him and bring him home. "Cleansing" from Caspar will assist in the process and conclude it. Your genius, your demon, your soul, Marius, will then be safe.

'But you and I know better, Marius. You and I know that out of your…friendship…for Milo and myself you will do what Milo wants done and what I want done for Milo's sake. You will bring Jeremy Morrison home. Even if you have first to get him into your power by doing to him what Milo evidently so much enjoys doing to him, and what he, Jeremy, so evidently enjoys having done.'

'Not my style, sir, or my taste.'

'Your style and your taste are to do what I command you because you are sworn to do it…under pain of my casting you away from me forever.'

'Perhaps, sir, I shall not need to go as far as…doing that to him. He may come with me because of my bright eyes.'

'Your bright, green eyes, little Egyptian? So he may. Now. Practical points. First, I shall have to obtain leave of absence for you for the rest of this quarter. Since you pay your own fees, albeit through your lawyer, this will not be difficult. If you are prepared to pay for education and board which you will not be receiving, who can reasonably object? I can add that I think your chances of a Scholarship at Oxford or Cambridge later on will be improved by travel in suitable regions now.'

'And my O Levels in December, sir?'

'Had you not heard? No, of course not, the news came through during the Exeat. Your O Levels are once again postponed, Marius, because the examiners are still demanding an automatic pass for all "disadvantaged" candidates and the Board still refuses to sanction this. What the examiners mean to do, of course, is to blight the career of promising boys like yourself by delaying and frustrating them. But in your case none of this matters in the slightest, as you will simply sit for a Scholarship when the time comes and no other examination very much matters. Also, of course, you need no financial help from the State, and even the Scholarship itself will only be honorific. You are utterly independent, whatever these malicious and half-witted dissentients may try to do to you. They will achieve only what they always achieve – horrible injury to the less clever and wealthy (and from their point of view more deserving), but not the smallest alteration in the lives of boys as brilliantly furnished as yourself.'

'Trains,' said Piero Caspar to Marius as they stood at the end of his garden in the Fens and looked along a dyke which went away from them in a straight line forever between two endless fields of nothing. 'I cannot drive: I loathe aeroplanes: I adore *i treni*, and so there is an end (to echo my poor old patron Ptolemaeos) of that.'

'I adore trains too,' said Marius: 'the kind of trains one eats in and sleeps in for night after night without getting out.'

'I'm afraid we're not going far enough for that. We shall have only one night *en route* to Rome, and I have a suspicion, little one, they will make us change in Paris.'

'Please don't call me "Little one" again.'

'What then?'

'My given name, "Marius". Or the Quaker mode: "Marius Stern".'

'Or just "Stern"?'

'Certainly. And you?'

'You call me anything you like. "Piero", "Caspar", "Brother Piero" (for I was once a religious, you should know), "my dear", "darling", or even "you slut". The only thing I cannot abide is "*Mister* Caspar". "Mister", these days, like "Signor" in Italy, is strictly for the lower-middle class. Let us walk along this dyke and I will tell you a thing, Marius Stern: I will tell you how for a long time I was a whore in Venice.'

'Why shall you tell me that?'

'Because you have "Future Whore" written all over your face, Marius Stern; and I should like to deter you if it is not too late.'

'Piero says we shall go by train to Rome,' said Marius to Carmilla, 'then South to Terracina, and wait there. It is a pleasant town for waiting, Piero says. One day Jeremy and Fielding's boat will anchor there or pass by on the sea – the fishermen will keep an eye open for us, Piero says – and then we shall confront them.'

'And when they refuse to return home?'

'I do not think Jeremy will refuse me after I have spoken with him. He will see that it is best.'

'Best? To spoil everything for a teenage blackmailer?'

'I have told you, Carmilla. I am doing this for love.'

'Not, I think, for love of Jeremy. Certainly not for love of me.'

'Try not to be bitter,' Marius said.

They both went to the window that looked down on to the South Door of the Chapel. There they held hands.

'You have made me let you go, on threat of exposing my brother-in-law and my sister,' said Carmilla: 'how should I not be bitter?'

'I have let you off much lighter than I might have done,' said Marius. 'I might have made you *order* them to come home. Instead, I have listened to your plea, and consented to go there myself.'

'Only because you are looking forward to an adventure. Yet that is good. Boys should look forward to adventures. They should look forward to nothing else.'

'I look forward to this, certainly. Piero says – '

'Come to bed, little Egyptian. Green eyes. The last time before you leave. My heart does yearn for you.'

'And mine for you, Carmilla.'

'Liar. Blackmailer,' she said.

'She is hoping,' said Raisley Conyngham, who was giving Marius luncheon in his chambers on the day before Marius' departure, 'that various factors and pressures will change your mind…that you will indeed confront Jeremy, but then break down and wave him on his way. But we have already been into that. Try not to become too dependent on Piero Caspar. He has a way with him.'

'He was once a sumptuous whore in Venice. Then a poor Friar.'

'And now he is a millionaire and landowning Esquire and a Fellow of Lancaster College. He has a way with him, as I say. Beware of him, little Egyptian. You are no match for him, except in one respect: you are sworn and dedicated. And so now – God's speed.'

'*God's* speed, sir?'

'Or the devil's. There is God, Marius, and there is Satan, who is also God. It is a question which is the greater God. If you look around you at the moment, you will see that the Satan-God appears to be triumphing. The winner is the True God, Marius. If the Satan-God prevails, then the worshippers of the other God are lost. Their decency, their faith, their love – will avail them nothing.'

'Is there no love in the Satan-God?'

'You know there is, Marius. You know his love. You are obeying it now. Do not betray it.'

'I like trains,' said Marius to Piero, as he gazed out of the window on the passing fields of Kent, 'as you do. But let us remember, Caspar, that we are rich enough to afford chauffeur-driven cars should we want them.'

'A hired chauffeur-driven car,' said Piero, 'means a hired chauffeur. These days a hired chauffeur expects to be accepted as a member of the party. They insist on…joining in. They turn surly and difficult if they are not allowed to join in. One can avoid their company at meals – though this is not always easy – but one cannot avoid their company in the car. Servants, Marius Stern, are always a nuisance like my man in the Fens, they are both deaf and dumb. I remember a servant in Venice who was kind to me; but there was a price. There is always a price.'

After a time, when they were passing the Castle on Folkestone Race Course,

'What happened to your foot?' Marius said. 'Were you born with it like that?'

'A cart ran over it in Syracuse.'

'I like Syracuse. Mummy took us once.'

'Thank your stars you weren't born in it.'

'It's done you no harm, having been born in it. Look at you now, Caspar.'

'Yes, look at me. Sneaking back into my own country with a fake passport.'

'Is there a risk?'

'None. The passport is not exactly fake. It is genuine in its kind. But it is a passport for someone who does not, to speak properly, exist.'

'Piero Caspar. They cannot arrest him if he has a genuine British passport. Presumably the person. . who did properly exist...the Whore of Venice and Brother Piero...has simply vanished.'

'He is in my heart. And I think in that of some others.'

'They cannot arrest your heart – or those of others – to take Brother Piero.'

'God can arrest my heart.'

'Which God?'

'What can you mean? There is only one.'

Marius sighed and began to explain. But Piero would not admit the Satan-God's equality. Well as he might be doing in the short run, Piero said, the Satan-God had been created by the True God and continued to exist only on the Latter's sufferance. He was, and must ever remain, inferior. Prove it, said Marius, and Piero could not, except by citing Writ.

In this manner they came to the Port of Dover, and the Sea.

PART THREE

The Ferryman

Hinc via, Tartarei quae fert Acherontis ad undas.
turbidus hic caeno vastaque voragine gurges
aestuat, atque omnem Cocyto eructat harenam.
portitor has horrendus aquas et flumina servat
terribili squalore Charon, cui plurima mento
canities inculta iacet, stant lumina flamma,
sordidus ex umeris nodo dependet amictus.
ipse ratem conto subigit veilsque ministrat
et ferrugunea subvectat corpora cumba,
iam senior, sed cruda deo viridisque senectus.

Hence a road leads to the waters of hellish Acheron. Here, oozing with mud and whirling to immeasurable depth, a seething vortex sucks in the sands and vomits them back into Cocytus' river. A loathly warden keeps these streams and currents, hideous in his filth, even Charon, over whose chin spreads a pelt of mouldy fungus. His eyes stare flame and a rotting cloak hangs from his shoulders. Unaided he punts the boat with his pole and trims the sail and in his black-blistered craft convoys the persons of the dead, an old sir now, this ferryman, but tough and green in age, wrought with the deathless fibre of the gods.

Virgil, *Aeneid* VI, 11.295 to 304;
Translated by S R

A friend of mine once told me,' Piero said to Marius, 'that Terracina had a remarkable number of barbers' shops, several of which were distinguished by the beauty of the twelve-year-old apprentices or assistants. Do you see any barbers' shops? Or beautiful apprentices?'

'These days,' said Marius, 'twelve-year-olds are not allowed to work. They are still at school.'

'This far south that would not prevent their being put to at least occasional use on the barber's floor. I worked part time for a barber at the age of seven.'

'That was in Sicily. And a long time ago.'

'Not so very long, Marius Stern. Here's the Cathedral. It is said to have a portico with an astonishing mosaic frieze above it. Do you see such a frieze?'

'I see a long strip of sackcloth and a notice which proclaims "*In Restauro*".'

'That is what I see. Let us sit here outside this café and admire it.'

'Admire what?'

'The place where the mosaic frieze would have been. Most of Italy is "*In Restauro*". One must get accustomed to using one's imagination...there being no twelve-year-old barbers' apprentices to distract us.'

'What did you do in a barber's shop at the age of seven?'

'I prepared old men to be shaved. I draped them and soaped them and brought in hot towels. Not many years before I should have been required to go beneath the drapes and pleasure them if they felt like it. Sometimes to suck them off.'

'But since that was no longer expected of you, you had,' said Marius, 'a comparatively sheltered childhood?'

'Not compared with yours. That portico is agreeable, mosaic or no mosaic.'

'My childhood, Caspar, was not as sheltered as you might think. I was subject to many temptations.'

'And I was subject to constant hunger and vicious blows, and every kind of what is now called deprivation. Later on, we shall exchange experiences. Now, I shall explain to you how we are to proceed in the matter in hand.'

'You have already done so. We are to wait here until Jeremy and Fielding come sailing by. If we do not see them, some kind fisherman will nevertheless inform us that they are here.'

'Long before they are here,' said Piero. 'Many of them have been given money.'

'They will take it and forget.'

'No, Marius Stern. This far south they know better than to trifle with Sicilians.'

'How do they know you are Sicilian? You are Mister Piers Pierot Caspar, the English millionaire, scholar and landowner. You have a passport to prove it.'

'They know I am Sicilian. Let us leave it at that. This coffee is deplorable.' Piero said three words to the waiter, who winced and whisked away their cups. 'You see?' Piero said. 'They will do better this time, I think. Now, where were we?'

'Waiting for the loyal and humble fisherfolk to warn us of the approach of Jeremy and Fielding.'

'We then talk to them,' said Piero. 'In particular you talk to Jeremy. You try to persuade him to return home at once, as is your wish. *Graz – i – e*,' he spelt out as the fresh coffee arrived. 'What shall you do if he refuses – as is Carmilla's wish and mine?'

'I shall…persuade him.'

'You will make love with him? That is surely not your way. You do not like men – in that fashion – I can tell.'

'I like you.'

'Not in that fashion,' said Piero. 'You would not make love with me.'

'I might…if I wanted something from you.'

'Then you would play whore. I have warned you against that. You must not play whore with Jeremy.'

'Why not?'

'Honour is why not.'

'You have played whore with many people.'

'Because I had no honour. Because I *was* a whore. All poor boys from Syracuse — and many rich ones too — are whores. They cannot be aught else.'

'I love it when you get excited. You mix your English up. You become Archaic or slangy.'

'Marius. Promise me you will not play whore with Jeremy.'

'I never said I would. *I* said I would persuade him. *You* started all this talk about whoring.'

'How shall you persuade him then?' Piero said.

'I shall be very tender of him. Then he will remember the time when I was a little boy and he took me to Newmarket and we won lots of money on an absurd horse called Lover Pie. He will remember things like that, and he will do as I ask.'

'This too is against honour.'

'Then how *shall* I proceed? Forbidden sex, forbidden sentimentality — how am I to approach him?'

'You are to look at him. You will see, very quickly, whether this voyage is doing him good, or harm. If it is doing him harm, you will say so and ask him to come home. But what harm can it possibly be doing him? Why do you wish to prevent him from completing it?'

'Because I've been charged to do so, Caspar, by those to whom I am bound.'

'What people? And how bound?'

'What people? The Master who has taught me everything I know. How bound? By my acceptance of his teaching, and by oath of obedience.'

'Such an oath is not binding- not in one of your age.'

'I choose, for the time at least, to be bound by it. Shall I tell you what my Master requires of me, should Jeremy not consent to come home?'

'To play whore?'

'Not exactly, no. Jeremy, as you may have heard, has developed a taste...an obsessive taste...for being buggered. That's what all the row in Oz was about. So if necessary I am to sodomize him. I *think* that I can make myself do it with conviction. He has a huge, kind bottom, just like his huge, kind face. I shall be very gentle with him. I shall ease my way up into him, and caress his penis at the same time. He has a large, long, rather flabby penis (so Milo Hedley tells me) which just at the last moment goes very stiff and comes very copiously. So when I feel that it is about to come, I shall cry out (even if I myself cannot come), "O Christ, Jeremy, I'm coming, O Jesus Christ", and he will cry out "O Christ, Marius, Christ, I'm coming too, O Jesus, Jesus Christ" (or something of the sort), just as he begins to squirt and shudder and spurt into my hand. Then he will be mine and will do as I Say.'

'You are just trying to excite yourself into imagining you will be able to do this. When it really comes to it, you will be small and soft as a snail. Quite useless.'

'And what will make me so? Some Sicilian spell of yours?'

'No. I shall use no spells on you, Marius. I shall simply teach you that you cannot use your friend in that way.'

'Go on then. Teach me – if you can.'

'Very well. For a start, I shall tell you a story about your dead cousin, Tullia. Baby Llewyllyn, as she used to be called...'

Fielding and Jeremy went to the Basilica of St Nicholas in the old town of Bari.

'The Guiscard again,' said Fielding.

'Again?'

'We went to that village in the north of Cephalonia, Huiscardo, the place where he died. This is where he lived. He began this Basilica.'

'You are muddling your Guiscards,' said Jeremy: 'it was Robert who died in Cephalonia, Roger that began this building. So what about them, in any case?'

'It is a long way from Cephalonia, all round the coast. We have come all that way.'

'No thanks to any Guiscard if we have. Though perhaps we should be grateful to that shrine on the rock just off Ithaca. The god there was on our side, I thought.'

'There are those twins of Jacquiz Helmutt's,' said Fielding: 'I wonder what they're doing here. My *God*, they are beautiful… and lust-making with it. Christ, those legs…under those short shorts. The groin look…'

'How truly lyrical you are today.'

Fielding and Jeremy waved to the twins, who waved back and turned away.

'They don't seem inclined to converse,' said Fielding.

'They were never inclined to converse,' said Jeremy.

'Still, in a foreign port, all this way from Cambridge…'

'The young like to be independent.'

'They are almost *too* young for that.'

'Anyway they've gone. Out through that doorway – '

' – The Lions' Doorway.'

'The young lions…Tell me,' said Jeremy, 'can't we somehow avoid Brindisi? Beastly place. Huge, squalid dock city. Nothing but thieves and whores. And nuns.'

'What made you think of Brindisi?'

'I've been dreading it. I went there once, with mother and Nicky, before she died and before Nicky…before Nicky's brain fell apart. In those days you used to go there in order to fly on to Corfu, which was what we were doing. We had to spend a night…in a hotel on the yacht quay. Just before Nicky and I went to bed, we were having a horrible little meal in the foyer, and a nun came in, collecting for something or other. She rattled the can right behind Nicky and frightened him, then looked at us both with hatred, little rich boys from England, you see, while she was begging for orphans or lepers or the blind or the maimed…'

'Lepers?'

'I don't know what made me think of them. Yes, I do. She looked leprous herself, that nun. Or what I think of as leprous, having never seen a leper. She was blotched dead white and livid yellow. My mother moved her on, but not before she too had received…that look of hate. I sometimes wonder if that nun put a curse on Nicky and mother, so that mother died young and Nicky's fine brain rotted in his head. But then why did she not put a curse on me too? Or perhaps she did; perhaps this itch of mine, this *oestrus*, is the curse she put on me.'

'Come,' said Fielding, 'you have not thought of that, or felt it, I think, for many days now.'

'It's the thought of Brindisi that's upset me. That cowled, leprous nun in the filthy hotel foyer.'

'We cannot avoid Brindisi altogether. But we need not linger there. We need not even go ashore, if you dread it so much. But if we don't we shall have to give it a very wide berth and sail by very quickly. The Italians get hysterical about naval security. They wouldn't mind us landing to be looked at; but they might not like it if we try to sneak round the edge of the harbour waters – they might think we were spying.'

'You'll try to find a safe course, though?'

'You're the Captain. You give the orders.'

'We shall not land at Brindisi,' Jeremy said.

'Dis *volentibus*,' Fielding added.

'First century,' said Piero. 'Majestic would you call them – these arches? Massive? Gigantic?'

'Colossal,' said Marius. 'The colossal and boring arches of a colossal and boring temple of a colossal and boring god. Jupiter. The most powerful and least attractive of them all.'

He turned to look down from the huge, high temple on to the pleasant little town of Terracina, as it sat by its pretty green gulf. 'That's better,' he said: 'life size. Nicely proportioned. Seemly.'

'I'm glad to hear you say so. Though you must not treat Jupiter quite so cavalierly. Some people still think he lives here on his mountain. He might snatch you for a second Ganymede.'

'I hate jokes like that about me,' fumed Marius.

'Yet you are prepared to describe to me, in detail, the way in which you would treat Jeremy to make him do your will. You are prepared to use somebody, I suppose, but not to be used – even by the king of the gods. Let me assure you, to use is quite as invidious as to be used and probably even more dangerous. That is the whole point of the story I have been telling you on the way up here – the story of your cousin, Baby Llewyllyn, and myself.'

'Then let us go through this thing again and get it straight. You and Baby Llewyllyn met in Venice, when she was thirteen and you were nearly sixteen. She went to have a pee while a guest in the Palazzo of the man who was at that time keeping you, and she didn't come back. You went to find her – and caught up with her on the roof, to which there was easy access as there was a kind of penthouse on it. She said she hadn't been able to find the loo and described to you, without leaving much out, how she'd taken her knickers down and squatted near the edge of the roof to piss. The idea of this little girl's straddling to make wee-wee – '

' – So close to the edge that she might have fallen off – '

' – So close that she was spraying her water over Venice – this idea excited you, Caspar. You couldn't do anything *then*, because very soon someone would have come after you, but the idea

149

stayed with you for many years. Meanwhile, you left your protector and became a Friar, and Baby grew up and married Lord Canteloupe, and you did not meet her again until you escaped from the Franciscan Convent in the Lagoon and made your way to England. Then at last you met Baby Llewyllyn again, Baby Canteloupe as she now was, and you found that she too had been excited by your encounter in Venice. She too had retained an inflammatory notion of what might have happened on that roof-top. So you decided, the two of you, to re-enact the incident, to re-enact what had actually happened and then pass on, by way of mutual stimulus and sexual speculation, to what might or could have followed, had there been time for it: But this was wrong; you say, this was indecent, and the results were disastrous. *Why* was it wrong and indecent, Caspar?'

'Because we were using one another's adult flesh to try to give body to sheer fantasy. When we first met, we were children. Had anything happened between us, it would have been, quite literally, child's play...erotic play. But what happened between us, between Baby and me when we met years later, was the ingenious recreation of corrupt minds. We were pretending, Marius, to be in a state of exploratory erotic delight, a delight to which we were no longer suited nor entitled. We used each other to make believe that we were children discovering desire, a little girl and a little boy made inquisitive by the process of micturation and experimenting with each other's parts to the point of a strange, new, intoxicating feeling. Orgasm. What is that funny white stuff coming out of you, Piero? Why are you sopping wet between the thighs, Miss Baby, why are your pretty knees trembling? All very proper in infants but not in mature men and women. An indecent abuse of mind and body. And what made it even worse, even more false, was that neither of us had been innocent even when we first met in Venice: I had... done what I had done...with many men and women; and Baby had received some very curious attention, disguised as instruction, from her mother. We should neither of us, therefore, have been discovering anything. So we were using each other, all those years later, to pursue a fantasy of a fantasy: to bring ourselves back to a state of enchanted sexual desire which in fact we could never have known even if we had had full time and opportunity on that roof-top in Venice, *could never have known*, Marius, because already, even so early, we had both been corrupted.'

'But what harm did you do? You pretended that you had first met each other before either of you knew desire, and that you had then discovered it. Untrue, of course; you couldn't have met each other while still in that state, and nothing happened between you when you did meet, so the pretence, as you say, is double, the fantasy of a fantasy: but nevertheless, Caspar, what *harm* did you get, did you or anyone else get, from that pretence? You played an entertaining sexual game together, you and my cousin Tullia, and that is all.'

'So one might have hoped. But she had begun to realize that we, the privileged, *were* just playing an entertaining – a refined and perverse – game, whereas there were countless others whose most basic sexual needs were never even acknowledged, let alone fulfilled. So the thing began to unhinge Baby. She was never the same again. Other things happened too that confused her; but it was what we did, I think, followed by her perception of its sheer futility and falsity, its wicked waste, its denial of needful and normal humanity, that ultimately led to her destruction.'

'Destruction?'

'She went to Africa, to settlements of lepers, to camps full of diseased men, to console them for their miseries with her body.'

'I heard that she became a nursing missionary.'

'In name. In fact she tried, not to cure sickness, but to alleviate pain and agony by the ministrations of her flesh.'

'Some might call her a saint,' Marius said.

'A prudent man does not desire saints among his acquaintance. Least of all that kind of saint.'

'What has all this to do with Jeremy and me? You're not suggesting that I might set him off on a similar course?'

'If you pretend to love him…in that particular way you described…when in fact you do not, he will sooner or later realize what you have done. The pretence, for a start, is dishonourable from one friend to another: its detection might lead to very unhappy results – though I should be surprised if they were as extreme as in the matter of Miss Baby. In any case at all, Marius, such behaviour in you would be indecent and unworthy. Am I plain?'

'I suppose so. I still do not understand how this game you played with Baby, when you were both grown up, could have sent her off…to do what she did…in Africa.'

'As I say, there were other elements in the matter. She felt, as so many do, that the world had been betrayed by a God who made it so full of torment and desolation, and that the best she could do was to console God's victims, in the only way she could.'

'I see. Anyhow, Caspar, in the name of decency, you tell me, I am not to sodomize Jeremy. Never mind. I have other ways of persuading him to come home with me.'

'What other ways?'

Ignoring the question, Marius turned to face the enormous arch behind him.

'If I apologize to Jupiter,' he said, 'for being rude about him earlier, perhaps he will assist me.'

'Perhaps he will. But I should not invite his assistance. By all means apologize to him – and then leave it at that.'

'You believe in the Pagan gods, Caspar?'

'I walk warily in their precincts.'

'Then why take the risk of even entering their precincts? Why did you bring us here?'

'To show you how kind and beautiful…how seemly…the world can be, when seen from the right viewpoint.'

'Yes,' said Marius; 'seen from a distance. Get close up and what have you? You look for a famous and beautiful mosaic, and you find a length of sackcloth.'

'One day the mosaic will be restored and replaced.'

'Possibly. But not before tens of thousands of people have come especially to see it – having *not* been warned by the Italian Board of Tourism of its removal – and have gone disappointed away, having spent much money, much effort, and in some instances the last remnant of their health and strength, only in order to be deliberately cheated and betrayed.'

'So our child will be born in late January?' said Canteloupe, as he walked with Theodosia by a stream that led across a meadow to a grove of lady-birch.

'My child and Marius' will be born in late January,' said Theodosia Canteloupe, 'or thereabouts.'

'You must forget about Marius.'

'Why? You have said that since the tests show that the child is to be a girl, you may wish Marius and me to try again for a son.'

'We need not necessarily call on Marius.'

'Yes, we need. He is the only one I could endure. The only one whom Teresa would allow to come to me. If I…submit… to Marius, Teresa will take a delight in the matter, because she has known and loved Marius since they were small. If I submit to anyone else – which in any case I could not – then Teresa will be sickened.'

'Very well. Let it be Marius – if I should decide to try again for a son.'

They came to the grove.

'Should you like to go in among the birches?' Canteloupe asked.

'Yes. I must see that the seat here is in good repair, in case it is fine enough to bring Teresa here when she comes for her Advent Absit in December.'

'Teresa is coming then?'

'Teresa is coming then, and for the Christmas holidays. You do not object...Canty?'

'Not in the least, my love. I am delighted you have such a clever and pretty child to amuse you...The wood of that seat by the pool is rotten. I shall have it replaced.'

'Thank you.'

'Luffham has sent me one of those benches which he has had made in memory of Jeremy.'

'Why does Luffham regard Jeremy as dead?'

'He doesn't go as far as that. He thinks that Jeremy has betrayed his early promise. It is that which he commemorates with these benches.'

'Jeremy never promised anything. He was a very attractive and amusing philanderer. He had a certain facility with words – generally with words borrowed from the works of others. And that was all.'

'You and Carmilla liked him well enough,' Canteloupe reminded her.

'We were very young. He was, at the least, amiable. Yes. We liked him well enough.'

'So would you like one of these "memorial" benches in here?'

'Why not? Thank you, Canty. But I still cannot imagine in what consists this "promise" Lufffham is commemorating.'

'He is commemorating his early hopes,' said Canteloupe. He opened a passage for his wife back through the close-set birches. 'When his elder boy, Nicky, began to decay in mind, Morrison – as he was then – set his hopes on Jeremy. Jeremy, so shining and wholesome, so affable and easy and courteous –'

' – So feeble,' said Theodosia, 'so feckless, futile and dishonest.'

'So treacherous?'

'No,' she said, as they came out by the stream. 'Never really treacherous, because he always warned one, often in so many words, that he was by nature one who glides away and passes by; so one could hardly impugn him when he actually did so. Deceitful he certainly was in other matters – deceitful about money, and also about love, pretending to resources which he did not have. Of course, as far as money goes, he now has enormous resources.'

'You wonder how he is getting on about love?'

'Yes. Carmilla thinks that his experience in Australia has made him ask important questions of himself. And she thinks that this voyage on which we have sent him may provide important answers. Nevertheless, she has allowed Marius to set out in an attempt to bring Jeremy home before the voyage is finished.'

'Why?' said Canteloupe. 'Why has she permitted Marius to interfere?'

'She hopes that Marius will see, before too late, that it is wrong, that it is indecent, to interfere in this, and so will break away from the influence that has persuaded him to interfere.'

'Raisley Conyngham?'

'Correct.'

'What does Carmilla hope for Jeremy in this?'

'That he will resist interference, if there is any, and will indeed be the person who instructs Marius why such interference is evil and evilly inspired, and will finally cause him to abandon Conyngham. Fielding Gray and Piero Caspar will be acting as Seconds, so to speak.'

'If Carmilla hopes for all that,' said Canteloupe, 'she is going to get at least one disappointment – '

' – And probably two. I know. Still, I think her plan was a good one Who knows, after all, what Jeremy might find in the course of his journey…his journey from Ithaca.'

When Tessa went to stay with the Canteloupes for her two-day 'Advent Absit', she arrived much earlier than she was expected (a muddle over the railway timetable) and was told that Theodosia was still resting. Normally, these days, she joined Theodosia in her long afternoon rests, but it seemed to her that it would look very pushy to thrust her way up to her Ladyship's bedroom at the very moment of her arrival; so she decided to walk for a while in the meadow by the stream that led to the grove of lady-birch.

As she left the house for the Rose Garden (through which she intended to approach the meadow) she met Leonard Percival, who was walking on two sticks.

'Visitor for you, Missy,' said Leonard. 'I left her by the Fives' Court.'

'Visitor? Her?'

'Get along and see for yourself. You should know the way by now.'

Tessa went back through the house to the Great Court and crossed this to the Fives' Court. Gat-toothed Jenny was waiting there for her.

'Jenny. How did you know I was here?'

'I didn't. I was at Warminster Station, collecting some kit from London. I saw you go along the platform to the Exit, and guessed where you was going. So as soon as I'd got my gear, I follows you. I want to tell you about Marius. I met him at the Duke's Arms at Farncombe some while back, like you suggested.'

'Was it all right?'

'Not really, no. He was uppity, offhand. But since he must have known by then that we were on different sides, I suppose I can't blame him. He must have thought I was shoving myself right at him. That, and interfering.'

'Was he unkind?'

'Not really. Just…what is the word? You'd know it.'

'Brusque? Perfunctory?'

'Perfunctory.' Jenny produced a fives ball. 'They've got a court like this where I'm working,' she said. 'They let us play.'

She started lobbing long shots from her right hand to her left, and back.

'Don't you wear gloves to play Eton Fives?' said Tessa.

'I don't need 'em.' Jenny played a shorter shot and mounted the step to field it. She patted the ball high up against the front wall, then struck it on the volley and killed it dead in the little box between the step and the buttress.

'*Brava*,' said Tessa.

Jenny came back to her at the rear of the Court. 'I don't like it much,' she said: 'I'm good at it, they tell me, but I don't like it. I play because Marius once told me that he played, and how he enjoyed it. Pathetic, isn't it?'

'No.'

'You had to say "No", love, but bless you all the same. Now look, Tess. I mustn't waste no more of your time. I know you're not keen to see me here.'

'I'm glad to see you anywhere.'

'Perhaps you will be when you've heard what I came to say. I came to tell you what Marius told me that afternoon in the Duke's Arms – that he was not going to do what Raisley Conyngham had planned for him but that he was planning something for himself. Does that make any sense to you?'

'Just a little, yes. He left School – suddenly and without saying "Goodbye". I think he's coming back next Quarter, but I don't even know that for certain. Then I had a letter from Thea – from Lady Canteloupe – which said that Marius had gone to meet his friend, Jeremy Morrison, at the suggestion of his sister, Carmilla.'

'That hardly means he's planned it for himself.'

'At least it means that he has decided on something that was not planned or ordered by Raisley Conyngham.'

'But did he have to *defy* Raisley Conyngham,' said Jenny, 'or was Raisley Conyngham quite happy with what Marius had decided?'

'I don't know.'

'It's important. If Marius went in spite of Raisley Conyngham's efforts to stop him, that would be grand, Tess. But if Conyngham was quite content for him to go…'

'I must say,' said Tessa, 'Raisley Conyngham looked quite happy with the world when I saw him in Chapel this morning.'

'There you are, you see. That means he's still in control.'

'Not necessarily. It just means that he's contriving to look happy. In any case at all, Jenny, Marius is now out of his immediate daily influence – which must be something to be thankful for.'

It had become dark while they spoke with one another. The Bell from the Campanile, Old Mortality, struck four.

'Good afternoon, ladies,' called Canteloupe, as he crossed the Great Court towards them. 'Thea is awake, Tessa, and longing to see you. And I must have a word with Miss Jenny here. Lucky she came just now.'

Tessa touched Gat-toothed Jenny's shoulder and disappeared through a door from a back staircase mounted to my Lady's chamber.

'Jack Lamprey,' said Canteloupe to Jenny. 'You knew him, I think?'

'How do you know about that? You don't even know who I am.'

'Oh, but evidently I do, don't I? I've heard how kind you were to Marius and Tessa at Ullacote in the spring. And how you took care of Captain Jack.'

'I liked him because he was good with the horse,' Gat-toothed Jenny said.

'He's falling to pieces now, at Ullacote. He needs you.'

'What can I do? I'm somewhere else now. I can't go back to Raisley Conyngham's stable at Ullacote, I can't, sir. Mr Conyngham wouldn't have me if I could. Anyways, why are you so bothered about Jack?'

'He was in my Regiment. He joined only just before I resigned; but I knew him.'

'Is it so, my lord? I see then. But I'll say it again, sir: what can I do?'

'My Secretary, Leonard Percival, knew Jack when he was a subaltern in Germany nearly thirty years ago. Percival was in a different Regiment, but Jack's Squadron was in the same barracks as Percival's Battalion, in a town called Göttingen. Leonard, who has a great talent for minding other people's business, says that in those days Jack had a passion for smoked salmon…a very rare delicacy then, but common enough now – so common that he may have got sick of it over the years. So what I want to know is this, Miss Jenny: is Jack still fond of smoked salmon?'

'Yes, sir. Or was when I was there. He has a side delivered by some Scotch firm every week. He used to share.' Jenny gulped. 'He was a sharing kind of man, you see. He'd take the bones out and lay it specially on a dish on the table in his room. And if you had to go in there to see him for anything, he'd share.'

'Yes,' said Canteloupe: 'we were good at sharing in our Regiment.'

'The pity was,' said Jenny, 'that it wasn't only his salmon he wished to share, but his snake.'

'I see…But you liked him?'

'Loved him in a way.'

'So you want to do the best for him now?' Canteloupe said.

'Indeed, sir.'

'Well then. If, one week, the firm in Scotland failed to deliver, you could take him a parcel of smoked salmon to make up. You wouldn't want to be seen at Ullacote, of course, after the way you left, but since you know the place so well you could go there in the winter evening, and make your way to his room, or to the kitchen perhaps, without anyone else's knowing…and leave a packed side of smoked salmon, addressed to Captain Jack.'

After a long time Jenny said:

'When will this be, sir?'

'This week. This evening. Now.'

'I see. Is it that bad with him, my lord?'

'Yes, Miss Jenny. All up. Another Army friend of his, much closer to him than I was – a man called Glastonbury – '

' – He used to come to Ullacote – '

' – I expect so. He told me about Jack. How badly Jack needs this present of salmon. He knew about you, Giles Glastonbury did, and he thought you were the best person to deliver it. Just drop it in, Miss Jenny. No one will ever know. The package will carry the label of the Scottish firm and the usual postage marks and so on.'

'It's a long pull from here to Ullacote. They'll be expecting me back at my place.'

'Not if I telephone. They know me well at your place. I'll tell them you're on an errand for me, and will be back much later tonight.'

'And what happens, sir, if Captain Jack…shares his fish with someone, as is his wont?'

'He will try it, I think, before offering it to anyone else,' Canteloupe said, 'just to make sure it is all right.'

'Yes, he will do that. He is a courteous man.'

'Once he has tried it,' said Canteloupe, 'he will dispose of it immediately. He will just have time to do this before it disposes of him.'

'Why did Canteloupe wish to talk to Jenny?' said Tessa to Theodosia Canteloupe as she tenderly scratched her bare back, then the bulge of her buttocks, then the slightly damp inside of the fissure between them.

'Canteloupe is thinking of buying some more horses. He will need another girl, a good girl, in the stable. He has made very careful enquiries about Jenny. He was impressed by what you once said of her, and by what Marius said, when asked about her, at the cricket here last summer.'

'I don't know that Marius really appreciates Jenny.'

'He seemed to, last summer. It will be all right, will it, if Marius should come here and happen to meet her?'

'Oh yes, I think so. Thea...exactly what is Marius going to Jeremy Morrison for?'

'Salvation. To win his freedom from Raisley Conyngham.'

'Raisley Conyngham...is looking quite unperturbed.'

'It is at least possible...that Marius will not pass the test. Then he will not be free of Raisley Conyngham.'

'Is anyone laying odds?' said Tessa.

'Carmilla says "even money". Myself, I'm laying six to four against Marius – against his passing the test. Teresa, put your head against my belly. If only it could have held the boy that Canteloupe wants. But they say it is a girl. Are they ever wrong, those people in laboratories?'

'I don't think so, Thea.'

'I wonder whether...Canty will make me try again. If so it must be with Marius. You will be with us both?'

Tessa shuddered.

'Oh yes. You will be with us,' Theodosia said.

'There's your parcel, Missy,' said Leonard Percival to Gat-toothed Jenny. 'I understand you know what's in it.'

'Smoked salmon. I only hope it's enough to keep Jack Lamprey happy.'

'Oh yes. I've taken no chances over that. One thing they teach you in Jermyn Street is to be thorough.'

'Jermyn Street?'

'Where I was brought up,' said Leonard, and did not amplify the topic. 'Now then: your contract.'

'Contract?'

'Detterling is about to buy some more chasers. Five or six, at the least. He wants you to train them.'

'Train them?'

'Don't keep on repeating me, Missy. It's like talking to a machine.'

'Sorry. Train them, you say – under whom?'

'He wants *you* to train them.'

'But...I haven't the qualifications. I haven't a licence.'

'Detterling and his old pal, Glastonbury, will see to all that. It'll be difficult, mind you, but they're very grateful to you for what you're doing to help Captain Lamprey, and so they'll make sure everything's in order. You can start on New Year's Day...if you will, Missy.'

'I will. The people I'm with now are very kind. They won't want to hold me back.'

'Good. I think you'll find Detterling's terms satisfactory. Unusually generous, in fact. I will say this for that stuck-up lot in Hamilton's Horse: they're always ready to shell out very handsome to help a friend. They're paying you very high, Missy, to bring *quietus* to Jack Lamprey. I doubt it's worth it, myself.'

'Jack Lamprey,' said Jenny, 'has deserved well of everyone that loves horses. And not so badly,' she added, 'of anyone that still believes in the human race.'

So Tessa has gone to that Lady Canteloupe for her 'Advent Absit', thought Maisie in Buttock's Hotel. And she'll go there for Christmas too. Leaving me alone. Why not? I'm only her old Auntie. Of course she can leave me alone.

If I told her I was really her mother, told the truth at long last, would she leave me alone then? Or would she come here to Buttock's for Christmas? She'd come here, that's what she'd do, she'd come home to her Mummy.

But I shan't tell her, not now, not ever. It would upset her. It would be mean. It would show I was jealous and spiteful. I'd get no pleasure of having her here. And I'd always be afraid lest someone would tell her, one day, how Maisie Malcolm was a whore that gave exhibitions and such. Then she'd know that her own Mummy used to lie there and let 'em all watch while the goose picked lentils and whatever out of her quim.

So. No Tessa for Christmas. No Fielding – off with that Jeremy again. No Marius – these days there never is. No Rosie: off to her mother in France. And none of her friends, no Jakki and no Carolyn – off to Corfu with their parents, and any old how they wouldn't come here unless there was Rosie or Tessa or Marius to play with. Why should they?

Well then. At least I've got all these books. Fielding showed me the way of it down at Broughton Staithe last summer, and now I know how to read them properly. A difficult thing to learn at my time of life (so they say), but then I was always interested, from some while back, ever since Tessa started bringing books home from school, set books for exams or just books to read in the holidays, and I've certainly got the hang of it now. So here's to a quiet Christmas, Jane Austen ('England's Jane') and Macaulay, and Boswell and Walter Scott; and though they may be a bit slow from time to time, they'll none of 'em play up awkward or answer back or get silly about some stupid boy or complain about the food.

Since Piero's Intelligence System indicated that there was still no sign of Jeremy's and Fielding's boat anywhere within a hundred miles of Terracina, he decreed that Marius and he could indulge in a day's outing. So they hired a car with a driver, who was to be trebly tipped on the condition that he never opened his mouth, and set out for Pompeii.

As they stood by the Casa di Plinio, Piero said, 'One is much tempted to moralize.'

'Pray don't,' said Marius.

'Not in the way you think. No talk of ever-lurking death and disaster, or of how they strike when least expected, thus denying the Impure in Spirit any chance of prior repentance. None of that. It is these remnants of *trompe l'oeil* that stir me to discourse. See here, Marius: a flat wall that is conjured into a vista of noble porticoes and deep gardens, in which peacocks strut and grinning satyrs couple with laughing nymphs – '

' – I see no peacocks strutting and no satyrs coupling with laughing nymphs. I see one jaded statue of an ill-favoured faun, and a thing crawling round the pedestal that looks like a mangy parrot.'

'But the spectacle is in any case more entertaining than a blank wall?'

'Certainly,' Marius conceded.

'Well then. My point is simply this. A certain type of artist – the late Rex Whistler, to take a more up-to-date example than we have here – can transform a dreary wall into a sylvan paradise or an enchanted city. But he must obey certain mathematical laws – the laws of perspective. So it is with human life. If you understand and apply certain laws...of *moral* perspective...you can pass through the dismal flat grey walls that surround you and into a magic country of woods and valleys and waters.'

'Very fancy talking, Caspar.'

'Not at all. Very practical, Marius Stern. When I was a boy, I was surrounded by insurmountable walls. I said to myself, "There is only one way out of this; you must become a rich man's whore." But then I remembered that most whores, however splendid their *debut*, end up broken and diseased. "What goes wrong?" I asked myself. The answer was simple: "Whores get greedy, they cheat, they are in consequence found out and thrown away. All that is necessary," I told myself, "is to behave honestly. Be an honest whore." Preserve a correct moral perspective, as I should say now, and the walls will dissolve to set you free and will *not* (as they have so often done for others) close in again and turn into a tomb to confine your oozing carcass forever.'

'And so you were a happy whore?' asked Marius.

'Passably so.'

'The other day, you warned me against whoredom.'

'Simply because you have the wrong moral perspective for the job. If you turned whore, you would not give yourself properly (which is one thing an honest whore has to do), you would grudge and you would cheat, and in no time the walls would close in again to trap you forever in misery and decay.'

'No worse than what happened to you. As I understand it you rebelled against your whoremaster and went to live in a dank and distressing convent with a bunch of imbecile and near gangrenous Friars. So much for your moral perspective.'

They walked to the centre of the Forum and then turned left for the Temple of Apollo.

'I had a great sorrow,' Piero said. 'A friend died. I did not rebel against my protector, I negotiated my release from him and went to live on the Island of Francesco del Deserto, where my friend was buried, and where there is, as you have just observed, a dank and distressing House of St Francis.'

'So you were once more immured. You had been exiled from the magic country and put back into the tomb.'

'Perhaps – for the time being. But I was thinking of my friend and I was resting...There are Diana and Apollo. The originals, I believe, are in a Museum in Naples. I am uncertain about Diana; but Apollo at least had the correct moral perspective – and moral dynamic.'

'The gods were not moral. Even Diana was chaste only out of contempt and disgust for priapic man.'

'That is why I do not think she had the correct moral perspective. Disgust and contempt have no part in this. But Apollo – he knew how to project himself out of darkness and into light.'

'Through divine power.'

'Through moral perspective – through obeying certain laws, above all the law of honesty,' said Piero, 'of seeing and saying things clear, and then of giving what you promise. When the time came, that was how I sought and found my release from the tomb of the Convent and came back to the shores of light.'

'How long did you stay in the tomb?'

'Only for as long as I wanted to. Long enough to think about my dead friend and to sort certain matters in my mind. Let us now go to the *Lupinare* and then return to the *Ristorante* here for lunch.'

'Who was this friend?'

'He was called Daniel Mond. A Jew – or half a Jew. He had been a Fellow of Lancaster. That is why I made for Lancaster when I finally flew from the Franciscan Convent. Daniel had moral perspective – sufficient to confront lingering death.'

'I see,' said Marius. 'And now I am meant to ask you, "Piero, Piero, what shall I do to be saved? Tell me this secret, which you have, and Mond had, and Apollo had – the secret that will bring me out of the tomb and into the green pastures." '

'It is no secret. It is under your nose, as it was under mine and Daniel's and Apollo's. Give what you promise and give it with your might – and, if you can, with your love, though I would agree that love is usually too much to manage.'

'I miss him, Balbo,' said Carmilla Salinger to Balbo Blakeney, the Steward of Comestibles and *Quondam* biochemist, 'I miss him most cruelly and in every conceivable way.'

'How many conceivable ways are there?' said Balbo Blakeney, as they walked along a path beneath which the willows drooped from the river bank into the old, cold, sluggish Cam.

'Physical, as I relish his stripling body. Mental and moral, as I am fascinated by his mind and his character. Personal, as I enjoy his company and his clever, bittersweet remarks. Possessive, as I would be his mother, to cuddle him in warmth and protect him from all harm.'

'You've got it bad, Miss Carmilla,' said Balbo: 'you're in love.'

'I never thought it could happen. Infatuation. Ate as the Greeks called it.'

'Not infatuation,' Balbo said; 'love.'

'Love is only for the lovable. For anyone else it is infatuation – like Pasiphae's infatuation with the Bull, or Narcissus' infatuation with himself. Marius is not lovable…until he proves himself to be so.'

'How shall he do that?' said Balbo, and huddled into his scruffy black overcoat against the churlish Fenland air.

'By letting Jeremy go on his way when he meets him. By not trying to bring him back. If Marius tries to bring Jeremy home, I cannot bear it for Marius, so unlovable will he have shown himself. If Marius succeeds in bringing Jeremy home, I cannot bear it for Jeremy, so feeble and faithless will he have shown himself. Balbo: I must make a plan to ensure that none of this can happen.'

'If you interfere now,' said Balbo, 'neither of them will be able to prove or show anything about himself. You must leave them to the test, Miss Carmilla, to the true test. You must not start rigging it, for or against either of them, not *now*.'

'And if they fail, one or both of them?'

'You will know where you are.'

'But such a failure would condemn them, ruin them; at least I might ensure that they came through well enough to be tested again another day.'

'And then you would want to rig *that* test too. What is the point of postponing the issue?'

'Because for as long as it is postponed, I can hope. And during the postponement they may become stronger, more fitted to meet the real challenge when it does come.'

'It's nothing much to do with me, Miss Carmilla. Take me out of the cold and give me tea.'

'If you will give me comfort, Balbo, give me counsel, in exchange…'

'…Now how would this be?' said Balbo, sipping his infusion in Carmilla's study. 'The test will come when they meet. Jeremy Morrison is striving towards his unknown goal. Marius is seeking to prevent him from following this good end, simply in order to gratify an evil Master, or so we all assume, whom Marius, in some sort, loves.'

'Is infatuated by.'

'Very well. But Atē, Infatuation, is quite as powerful as any love. What I propose, Miss Carmilla,' said Balbo, his face shrivelled as a dying satyr's, 'is that so far from rigging or postponing the test (there being no desirable outcome of either process) you ensure it happens as soon as possible. Time will only dull Jeremy's purpose and his willingness to search: time will only turn Marius sour with Piero's saws and instances.'

'Piero telephoned a day or two ago. He thinks he is making some headway.'

'Exactly. But he has only to make headway a yard too far, and he will become importunate and lose Marius. Therefore act now. Both Jeremy and Marius are probably as well disposed to prove themselves…lovable…as ever they will be. Do not fudge this thing, Miss Carmilla; that will prove nothing and at best achieve injurious delay. See that the Test is fair; see that it happens as soon as may be. I would suggest some such device as this.'

When Raisley Conyngham heard that Captain Jack Lamprey, his private trainer, was dead down at Ullacote, apparently of food poisoning, he arranged to transfer his horses to a stable near Taunton. Then, reflecting that after this mishap it was surely time that cause be given him of pleasure or rejoicing, and that his greatest desire, now as ever, was for the total subordination of Marius Stern, he crept about to find what news he could of Marius' mission and Jeremy's response.

Having encountered Tessa Malcolm at the top of the steps down to the School Fives Courts, he said, 'Kiss and be friends, Teresa? I am sorry about what happened in the Spring.'

'Too late, sir. I shall neither kiss nor be friends again with you, now or ever. But that is not to say that I shall be uncivil.'

(Nobody, she thought, needs gratuitous enemies.)

'You have been to Lady Canteloupe for the Absit?'

'Sir.'

'Is there news of Marius?'

'None. I have a Fives Match, sir. Pray excuse me.'

As he followed her down to the Fives Courts, Raisley saw that the match was to be Tessa with Rosie Stern versus Jakki and Carolyn Blessington. Since Rosie was far the worst player and Tessa far the best, this evened things out. Pondering why Rosie should be so inept at ball games when her brother Marius performed so superbly at all of them, Raisley Conyngham walked by the Green for a while and reached the conclusion that Marius must favour his mother (the dashing and physically facile Isobel) and Rosie have inherited more of her father; for whereas the late Gregory Stern had been a gallant horseman (so he had heard) and ridden with the King's Guard, he had been a shambling mess when it came to any other sporting activity.

After an hour or so, Raisley Conyngham returned to the Fives Courts to watch the girls – pink, sweaty, besweatered – as they ambled away for home. He saluted them and passed by, but then lurked and followed until they separated to go to their respective *Domos Vestales* to shower themselves and put on fresh clothes. He caught up with Rosie on a narrow path that led round the rear of the Headmaster's Lodge.

'A moment, Miss Rosie, if you please.'

'Yes, Conyngham of Ullacote?'

'What word of Marius?'

'No word to me, Conyngham of Ullacote. Have you had none?'

'No, nor expect none for the time. But I wondered if he had perhaps sent…to the lady his sister?'

'Marius and I are not close just now, 'Squire Conyngham. But we shall be close again, I think, when Marius puts by childish things.'

'Childish things, Miss Rosie?'

'You, Conyngham of Ullacote, you and Master Milo Hedley. I had heard all about this before ever I came to this School. My friend Teresa Malcolm and my friend Jakki Blessington told me. To my mind, Ullacote, you and Milo Hedley are like the bad fairies in a pantomime – the floppy-horned Demon King and his fumbling red-nosed equerry. Clowns. Childish things.'

Rosie's black hair, which she had bound up for the match at Fives but had later loosened, fell almost to her waist, and her long, skinny legs began to quiver into a dance.

'I don't think you quite appreciate what I am doing for Marius,' said Raisley Conyngham: 'I am teaching him…to win without effort a fine share of the world's prizes.'

'At worst, then, witchcraft, warlockry. At best, you are trying to turn him into another red-nosed equerry,' said Rosie, skipping in a small circle (very small, because of the narrowness of the path) round Conyngham, who wore a long cloak that fell almost to the ground. 'Look at you, in that bizarre get-up. Not even a proper warlock, just a joke conjurer,' she shouted as she danced, 'a comic cutpurse, a mountebank, a charlatan. I can't understand why Marius hasn't seen through you long since.'

'Then let me enlighten you, Miss Rosie. Marius loves me and I love him, each in our fashion. Neither his fashion nor mine has aught to do with pleasuring on the one hand nor moonstruck romance on the other: his has to do with devotion, mine with instruction, his with obedience, mine with service; both with faith and faithfulness. Marius is bound to me, Miss Rosie, and I am bound to him. Say what you will, little Virtue, little Jewess,

"'Tis thus the matter is:
My true love has my heart,
And I have his."'

Then Rosie stopped capering because she thought this was probably true. She had made a brave effort to ridicule Raisley Conyngham, to taunt him that all he had of Marius was the captious and transient hankering of a little boy. She had thought and much hoped that this might be so; now she knew that it was not. She flickered away into the dusk.

As for Raisley Conyngham, while having tea in his chambers after his confrontation with Rosie, he reflected that, although Rosie's taunt was untrue, and although it could never become true (such was his hold), it was nevertheless time that the solemn *entente* between Marius and himself were cemented by a victory, a victory for himself in the precise exaction of what he willed, and a victory for Marius in its precise performance. But as to Marius' present mission, there was little that he could do now. Marius had gone, with his blessing. Perhaps, he thought, he had been a little too quick to accept that Piero Caspar was to accompany him; but he had warned Marius against the capabilities of Caspar, and was certain in his mind that Marius, the princely Egyptian, would not be seduced (in any sense) by Piero, the whore, the booby friar and the wop. He could, of course, send Milo to follow and observe them. Yet nothing, he thought, was to be gained by this; for it was clear to him that Marius, while he still affected to respect Milo as a junior should respect his senior, was already Milo's superior in all things, and that, therefore, if Marius could not resist the suasions of Caspar, there was certainly nothing that Milo could do about them. His own (Raisley's) intervention in Italy, in any case difficult to effect at this stage in the School Quarter, would be tactless and unproductive. The time had come, thought Raisley, for a true encounter, for a proving of mettle, for Marius to stand alone against the Enemies, which others called Chivalry and Decency but which Raisley hated as Hypocrisy and Delusion. Such a stand, if successful, would confirm that Marius was now equipped to subvert the fatty righteous and (in the not too distant future) ransack their treasuries. A definite Test there must be at some stage, thought Raisley Conyngham: let it be now.

'The finest Greek temples are to be seen in Sicily,' said Piero to Marius. 'The next finest in Italy, here at Paestum. This is the Temple of Hera (mid-sixth century BC). Note the barrel-shaped and fluted columns, without plinth.'

'Why should I note them?' Marius said.

'As typical of the period.'

'Why should I care about the period?'

'Because you are a fastidious person and like to have things tidily arranged in your mind.'

'When I remember this place, it will not be for this temple or any temple. It will be for the sedge and the marsh that slowly seep away to the sea.'

'In spring there would be flowers and herbs in this meadow. Asphodel and many aromatics. Even now there is the evergreen oleander.'

'I prefer the salt marsh.'

'Then you are a very morbid boy. But if you must be morbid, will you not admire these cypresses?'

'Even those have too much of self-advertisement about them, like you, Piero. The salt marshes keep their counsel.'

'Do they indeed? I should have thought they just sulked... This is another Temple of Hera. Although it is called a Temple of Neptune or Poseidon, it was in fact dedicated to Hera.'

'How do you know?'

'Because the Green Michelin says so,' said Piero. 'I read it before we came. That was where I got all that about Asphodel and so on.'

Marius laughed and his mood lifted.

'Why did you make me pack this morning?' he said. 'Why have we brought our bags with us?'

'Because we have left Terracina. I have hired this car and this driver (once again, heavily bribed to maintain total silence) to bring us to Brindisi...the antique Brundisium.'

'Virgil landed there on his way back from Greece?'

'He did. And died there. Very soon Jeremy and Fielding will land there. They have not come as far as I thought. We cannot go on waiting while they make the entire journey round the heel of Italy and up to Terracina.'

'How do you know they will land in Brundisium?'

'Luigi, my fisherman ally in Terracina, went to Bari to squabble with his fifteen cousins about a legacy. While there, he saw a boat in the yacht harbour with two eyes on the bow and no name.'

'Not all that unusual.'

'He also saw two men, unmistakably English, who fit the description I gave him of Jeremy and Fielding. They were waving to two beautiful children, a boy and a girl. In the Basilica.'

'What an odd scene.'

'Odder than you know. The two children, from Luigi's account, resemble very closely the twin children of my new Provost, Sir Jacquiz Helmutt. Just what business would *they* have in Bari? But I shall say nothing of this for a time. Luigi glimpsed them only very briefly, and may have described them wrongly; silence will be the sensible thing in *that* affair, I think.'

'How long before Jeremy and Fielding reach Brundisium?'

'Brindisi. How would you feel if I called Richborough "Rutupiae"?'

'I shouldn't mind in the least.'

'We shall be in Brindisi before they are. The weather down the east coast is bad. They will move very slowly – not at all, perhaps – for several days. This is the Temple of Ceres, so called, really erected in honour of Athena.'

'Athene. How do you know,' said Marius, 'that Fielding and Jeremy will anchor at Brundisium?'

'Brindisi. If they don't, we shall find them a bit further down the coast.'

'Can't we wait further down the coast anyway? Brindisium is a disgusting place. Jeremy once told me about it – he went there when he was little to catch a connection for Corfu. I shouldn't think he'll want to stop there at all.'

'One cannot tell. They may have to put in there. We can do no harm by going there first. In any case you should see the place.'

'Why? If Jeremy says it's disgusting, why should I want to see it?'

'Because it contains many very poor boys such as I was in Syracuse.'

'Stop pitying yourself. Syracuse is a jolly nice place.'

'Only those parts of it that those like you would visit Much of it is as horrible – almost worse – than Brindisi. So I wish you to see Brindisi and see the boy that I was in Syracuse.'

'Why should I want to do that?'

'Because I wish you to do that,' Piero said. 'You are a clever, beautiful boy, Marius, and you are an enchanting companion (when you choose to be); but you are lacking in charity. When you see what I was, when you see boys smiling at you with the snarl of a whore in the smile, the way I used to smile until Daniel Mond taught me not to, then you may learn a little charity – if it is not too late.'

'Another letter from Earle Restarick,' said Jacquiz Helmutt to Marigold over breakfast at Grantchester, 'about the twins.'

'True or false?'

'Simply another little exercise in fiction, to cover us in case someone should come enquiring. You know as well as I do that there was never any real hope of Earle's catching sight of the twins. Why should they go anywhere near him? They have their own interests, one must suppose, and the whole of the Mediterranean – the whole of the world – in which to pursue them.'

'I know, Jacquiz. I do think that they might – that they ought to have sent some sort of message by now. They must know that we're anxious.'

'I don't think that they are much bothered by that sort of consideration. Another problem now arises,' said Jacquiz, who was already examining another letter: 'when would you wish to move permanently into the Provost's Lodging in the College?'

'I don't wish to move in there at all.'

'I'm afraid we've got to. Preparations have been made to fit it out for a married couple with a family – obviously predicating the presence of the twins. It will look odd, and ungrateful, if we just skulk out here at Grantchester as if I were trying to distance myself.'

'What does Len say?'

'Len says that we must give a definite and not too remote date for moving in, and then stick to it. He suggests a day early in the New Year. Meanwhile, the Lodging will be available for the customary offices of the Provost's Christmas hospitality, but we needn't sleep there unless we wish.'

'Why not move in now, now and be done with it?' Marigold said. 'What difference between here and there? In either place there will be two empty beds in the Night Nursery.'

'It's really a matter of tactics,' said Helmutt: 'I've got a grip on that College and I don't intend to let go. On the one hand I must start living inside it fairly soon; on the other, I do not wish to appear too concerned about the matter. As Len says, early January will do very well.'

'Then so be it,' Marigold said.

'If we are to sail past Brindisi without going into it,' Jeremy Morrison said to Fielding Gray, 'we must set course further out to sea.'

'Yes. I don't like the look of that sky.'

'And I,' said Jeremy, 'don't like the look of the shore hereabouts. Not a building in sight. Deserted. Just marsh and quicksand, I shouldn't wonder.'

'I like the look of that shore,' said Fielding, 'more than I like the look of that sky. Anyway, we haven't time to be clear of Brindisi before nightfall.'

'We could sail in the dark for a while,' said Jeremy; 'just this once.'

'Why are you in such a hurry? You insisted that we should leave Bari before the weather was settled; and now you want to sail straight out into a storm – and then on through the night.'

'What storm?'

A diagram of silver veins was flicked on over the clouds in the east and flicked off again. After some seconds there was a low growl.

'There you are. It's only fifteen hundred hours and the light is quite murderous. We must put in to that shore.'

'That storm cloud is drifting north,' said Jeremy. 'If we set course south-east, it will take us clear of the storm *and* of Brindisi.'

'Jesus Christ, Jeremy. What *is* your hurry?'

'To be safely past Brindisi. I hated it when I was there years ago, and I've hated the memory ever since. I can't get over the feeling that…that there's something nasty waiting there for me.'

'Don't be ridiculous. Anyway, if we put into this shore now, there will be nothing to stop us sailing right round Brindisi tomorrow or whenever the weather clears. We bought plenty of everything in Bari.'

Another, larger and brighter, map of veins appeared in the east. At the same time, the declining sun was shining down on the shore to their west.

Jeremy surveyed the shore through his binocular.

'There's nothing there, Fielding; nothing. Just a green sort of ooze as far as I can see…with this thing.'

Fielding took the binocular; he held it vertically in one hand and put the bottom glass to his one eye.

'There is what could be one of those Trulli things right down towards the south,' he said.

'Trulli things?'

'Special kind of building like a beehive which they used to live in round here…and there are two more beyond it. They generally come in groups of three or four. The Belle Arti preserves them.'

'On a shore like this?'

The sun shone on the green marsh a mile away. A savage squall of rain, apparently falling from nowhere, blotted out the view. The cloud, spreading like a stain, was moving west towards them as well as north. A boat similar to their own, white, with two eyes in the bow and no name, passed them at ten yards' distance to starboard. An oil-skinned figure waved from its little bridge.

'He wants us to follow,' said Fielding.

'No choice now.'

It was black all round them. There was an explosion of God knew what less than a furlong to their left. A sort of flaming football sizzled across the sea between them and the boat ahead.

'Lights,' yelled Fielding. 'Lights on, like his. Or we shan't be able to keep sight of each other.'

Jeremy fumbled about. A search light came on above their heads. In its beam they could now see two oil-skinned figures, so close they were almost fused together, on the bridge of the other boat. One of them waved again, a forward, circular, rather gangling movement of its entire arm, like a very young officer giving his platoon the order to charge. The sea swelled hugely but did not foam or break. The rain, slanting slightly from the east, went straight through Fielding's and Jeremy's elegant blue blazers and turned them into dish cloths.

'Follow,' yelled Fielding, 'follow. Follow the twin Dioscuri.'

Marigold dreamt that her twins were sailing in a quinquireme out of the Port of Tyre. They were standing side by side, very close, on a platform in the stern behind the Master of the vessel, who sat on a throne. On a second and smaller platform, below the Master's, a brown naked man beat a slow measure on a deep drum.

Marigold was lying on a couch by the window of a room on an upper floor of a building near the end of the quay. As the quinquireme passed, Marigold waved to her twins, who smiled, albeit gravely, and waved back, with curious circular movements of their arms, which seemed to indicate the direction in which they were sailing, to the west.

Marigold watched until the quinquireme cleared the harbour bar. She heard the drum beat quicken. Although she was crying, she was happier than she had been since many days; for at last her twins had thought of her, and sent her a message, that they were in good case, well and sternly engaged in going about their business – whatever that might be.

'Brindisi next stop,' said Fielding to Jeremy, 'whether you like it or not. We have no choice.'

From the outside stairway of the central and largest of a group of three *Trulli* half way up, they looked on to a grey beach of mud, then out over a calm black sea and into the risen sun. There was a channel down the beach to the sea: at the near end No Name was moored.

'Where did they go,' said Jeremy, 'after sending us up this channel?'

'God knows,' Fielding said. 'What I know is that three quarters of our stores have been ruined by sea water, that we have no dry clothes to change into, that this absurd *Trullo*, if that's the correct singular, is an abomination – '

' – You ought to be hellish grateful for it. It was at least shelter of some kind. But for this blessed Trullo, we'd be dead of exposure.'

'We shall be dead of pneumonia or starvation unless we run straight into the harbour at Brindisi and set ourselves to rights.

'We must get to a hotel, get dry, get some proper rest – '

'Not to the hotel on the quayside,' droned Jeremy: 'please.'

'There is a Jolly hotel in Brindisi these days. In the main square. I looked it out in the Italian Michelin,' said Fielding, 'some time back. Not quite *us*, perhaps, but reliable.'

'I still don't want to go into Brindisi.'

'Perhaps you'd prefer to die of an ague?'

'You're right of course,' said Jeremy miserably. 'God, I do get bored with your being right.'

They crossed the mud in bare feet, their dark grey trousers clinging horribly to their calves.

'Let us pray that none of the sea got into the carburettor. Or the fuel tank.'

But No Name started faithfully. As the boat nuzzled down the narrow channel, Fielding turned to look at the three *Trulli*, in the best preserved of which they had passed a bitter and distressful night, trying and failing to light a fire from a few spars of damp wood that were leaning against one wall of the otherwise unfurnished chamber on the ground floor, clinging to one another for warmth but only wringing out water from each other's clothes and working it deeper into each other's flesh.

'The origin of these things is said to be prehistoric,' said Fielding: 'in the Middle Ages they were often inhabited by schismatic Christians who wished to keep out of the way. I should have thought this lot here would have been sitting ducks for Saracen pirates.'

'Better that,' said Jeremy, 'than falling into the hands of the Inquisitors. Really, why did people make such a fuss about religion? What did it matter to any sane man whether Christ was of like substance to God or the same substance? All bigotry and fanaticism.'

'Bigots and fanatics are back in business again,' said Fielding. 'Those bloody Moslems. Everyone thought fanaticism was a thing of the absolute past – until out popped the Ayatollahs and their gangs of Schi'ites. The Shah may not have been exactly one's best thing, but at least he had the sense to put that lot down.'

'Until they put him down,' Jeremy said.

They cleared the shallows and turned south down the coast for Brindisi.

'Two hours should bring us there,' said Fielding, looking over a chart. 'Entrance *there*, dear boy, then veer right, as shown by markers, to the yacht harbour.' He scrabbled about in a niche. 'Chocolate?' he said to Jeremy. 'Apparently unspoiled. Sporting and Military. Very better-making.'

'No thanks,' said Jeremy, and shivered.

'Trouble already? The sun should start warming you up in a little while. And the engine.'

'Not the sort of trouble you mean. "Thou would'st not think, Horatio, how ill's all here about my heart." '

' "Nay, good my lord." '

Fielding hugged his friend from behind, to soothe him. After a while Jeremy said –

'Do it to me, Fielding. Do it. You never have. Do it now, like this. Please. It's been so long since I had anybody.'

'I can't.'

'Help me, Fielding.'

'I *can't*. Don't you understand? I cannot, any longer, do what you ask...to anybody.'

'Oh dear. I do long for it. I need all the comfort I can get, going to this horrible place.'

'I'll take care of you. We shan't be there very long, Jeremy. I'll take care of you. You'll see.'

But Jeremy continued to shiver and sob as he stood at the wheel of No Name.

Marius Stern looked down into the great gorge beneath Matera. Piero, in whom, during the day's drive, long periods of listlessness had alternated with frantic little bursts of nervous prattle, was clearly off colour and had gone to take a late siesta. Or so Marius thought; but, 'Such a deep ravine,' said Piero's voice behind him. 'I shouldn't jump into it, if I were you.'

'I have no such intention.'

'Then don't walk too close to the edge – just in case you feel dizzy and topple in.'

'Such nonsense, Piero. If I toppled from here it would be on to that bank just beneath. At worst I should slide into the next street below it.'

'But there is a place, not far from here,' said Piero, 'where a spur of land juts right out over the chasm. It is fenced off, of course, but the fence is not very formidable. Any fool could get through – and walk to the tip of the spur. Would you like me to show you?'

'No thank you, Piero. I should like you to order a decent dinner – if such a thing is to be had in this beastly place – while I go and change.'

'I'm afraid the water in the hotel isn't very hot.'

'I don't mind lukewarm water.'

'Ah: neither hot nor cold: Marius the Laodicean.'

It took Jeremy and Fielding longer than they had supposed to reach the yacht harbour at Brindisi. There were several early setbacks. Twice the No Name's engine cut out and needed a lot of inexpert tampering and clumsy cleaning of points. The wind was still from the south-east and delayed them. Fielding made at least two foolish errors in reading the charts and in putting them on course for the entrance of the harbour. Luckily the sun and the warmth of the engine dried them (more or less) as Fielding had hoped, and he found some tins of Spam (oh, shades of 1944) and undamaged packets of Rusk Rolls. All in all, then, they arrived in their berth in better nick than they might have expected; but by this time it was dusk.

'Lock everything lockable,' said Jeremy. 'The police are quite worthless here. Worthless if not downright corrupt.'

'Where's the nearest taxi rank?'

'If we go along the quay, past that ghastly hotel, we should be able to find one to take us up to the Jolly.'

But this was not to be. Out of the shadows came two figures in oilskins, their faces invisible within their deep sou'westers. One took Fielding's left arm and the other took Jeremy's right arm, in a grip that might not be resisted, and led them towards the mouth of a narrow alley, down which they must proceed in Indian file.

After a passable dinner, achieved through the power of Piero's Sicilian manner, Piero and Marius went to see the baroque church of San Francesco, which was still open, late as it was, in honour of Advent.

'But they think more of the New Year than of Christmas,' Piero said, 'and more of the Magi than either.'

'Funny. I thought the Italians adored the image of the Mother of God with her new-born Child on Christmas morning.'

'They adore the Mother of God. The actual Child is another matter. Italians remember how their mothers kept them quiet, when they were fractious, by playing with their little pricks. It embarrasses them to think of Mary doing this to the God-Child – though many painters get very near to showing her at it – and so Mariolatrists, a strong majority of the church in Italy, tend to leave Jesus Christ out of the reckoning.'

Jeremy was in a closed litter, borne by bearers whom he could not see and accompanied by the two figures in oilskins, who were walking one to the right of the litter and one to the left. These he could see through glass panels in the sides of the litter, which in other respects resembled a very spacious and comfortable coffin. He was lying on a long cushion, with a light silk covering over him. His blazer and slacks had been replaced by pantaloons and blouse, also of silk. He had no idea how he had come to be there. He remembered feeling faint in the alleyway into which he and Fielding had been conducted, and then nothing more. Fielding was now nowhere to be seen.

They were, it appeared, ascending. To either flank of Jeremy's palanquin were rows of poor, ruined buildings, utterly deserted. Not so much as a pi-dog was visible. The oil-skinned figures both walked on narrow pavements which proceeded uphill about a foot clear of the crumbling façades which they passed.

'I am the spirit of Virgil,' said a very low, light voice within the palanquin, 'and you are my body. Together we are Virgil, the poet, and we have sailed from Greece to Brundisium. You, my body, are very ill; this weakens the link between us, but I think that you can still hear and understand me. We are being brought from the quayside to the quarters allotted us by the servants of the Emperor. There a physician and others, both friends and enemies, will attend us.'

And indeed Jeremy felt very ill, though of what he could not have said. He was in a high, dry fever, he thought, body throbbing, limbs heavy, chest burning. He was, with it all, overwhelmingly tired; and so, despite his manifest and manifold discomfiture, he dropped suddenly into a black sleep.

'Would you come and sleep with me, Piero Caspar, if I invited you?'

'Why should you do that? You do not like men or boys, not sexually.'

'I am inviting you out of sheer curiosity,' Marius said.

'Using me. Not a respectable motive.'

'At the same time, I rather love you, you know.'

'And I rather love you, *Mario caro*. If we wish to go on rather loving each other, we shall stay out of each other's beds.'

Jeremy awoke in a long and barely furnished room. He was lying on his back in a high bed; on either side of him, just below the level of his head, was one ample and seigneurial chair (the ends of its arms ornamented with a lynx's head in ebony), behind each of which stood one of the oilskin-clad figures, their faces still concealed in the depths of their cavernous headgear. They were both of medium height, Jeremy noticed, giving an impression, from their movements, of being sturdily but gracefully built. From time to time, one or other of them walked down past the bed in order to peer through an arched and unglazed opening, about eight feet tall and three feet in breadth, its base being about a yard and a half from the floor and not quite parallel to it, which faced Jeremy from the far end of the chamber. What either of the figures could see through the opening puzzled Jeremy, as all he could observe was totally opaque darkness, unrelieved by planet, star or moon. Light within the room, dim but sufficient, was given by two flambeaux, one in the left hand of each of the oil-skinned figures.

'The physician will be here shortly,' said the low, light voice, close to Jeremy's left ear. 'He is a conceited and pretentious Greek from the Medical School at Epidauros. He will be able to do nothing about your fever, but he will provide a draft to soothe your stomach.'

And sure enough, a stocky little man, showing a great deal of hairy leg beneath a saffron garment that ended well above his knees, and jutting a silly, spiky beard, now entered the apartment from a door in the wall, which Jeremy had not so far noticed, to the right of and just behind the bed. He held up a crystal goblet of some fizzing liquid, which he gave to Jeremy to drink. Jeremy, in his thirst, drank it off gratefully, noting that the taste was somewhere between sherbet and alka-seltzer. Almost at once his stomach felt easier, and though his fever still baked him as in an oven, he felt a certain curiosity about what was to happen next.

'The problems are quite clear,' murmured the voice. 'We, Virgil the poet, are near to death, which will occur as soon as I, the spirit, am compelled to leave you, my body. This will not be long now. So: first, there is some disagreement about what should become of my epic, *The Aeneid*. I, as you may know, would wish it destroyed, because there are many clumsy passages in it, which we are too weak, you and I, to revise. What is more, I am doubtful of its message: this is that the Fates (not the Gods but the Fates – the distinction is important) have given Rome to the descendants of Aeneas of Troy to be their city forever, and have caused them to go forth from Rome in order to conquer with glory and rule with justice the greater part of the known world. Time was when I would have exulted in this notion; but as I grow older, and look upon the persons and demeanour of some of Aeneas' successors, I become, as I say, doubtful. However, as to this, the first of our problems, there is no point in disturbing ourselves; for the servants of the August Caesar have a copy of *The Aeneid* in their possession, and since Caesar very much likes the idea of being, so to speak, the Champion of the Fates, it will most certainly be much re-copied and widely distributed. There is simply nothing to be done about this, so one may just as well forget it.'

'And the other problems?' said Jeremy.

One of the oil-skinned figures moved lithely and easily to the window, peered out through the funnel of his headpiece, then moved back to stand behind his chair. Neither had paid any attention to the voice of Virgil nor to the voice of Jeremy, though the latter, at least, must be audible to them.

'There is only one remaining problem. It greatly involves you, O faithful body which I must leave so soon. You will recall, I think, that the second of our Pastoral Poems, or Eclogues, concerns a shepherd, Corydon, who loves a beauty called Alexis, who in turn is the favourite of his rich master and therefore will have nothing to do with the crude courtship of Corydon. Corydon is reduced to wandering the wild woods –

– *Tantum inter densas, umbrosa cacumina, silvas*
Assidue veniebat –

and singing the song of lament and pleading which I have composed for him.'

'I remember the poem well. It is one of my favourites.'

'Then you will help me to save it?'

'Save it, Master?'

'Do not call me "Master". You are my body, not my slave. Yes, save it. I told you that enemies as well as friends will visit us here. There is an enemy who is trying to claim authorship of this poem and of one other of the Pastoral Poems – the one about the song of Silenus to his pupils.'

'How could this enemy...claim authorship of your work?'

'By getting us to sign a death-bed declaration that he was, indeed, the author of these poems.'

'And just how could he get us to do such a thing?'

'First, by blackmail. Like all other men, I have done many things of which I am ashamed – but not so ashamed that their revelation would much affect me. And in any case I am soon to be dead, so what care I if the world learns that once I killed a common sailor who tried to rob me, here in this very city, and kicked his body into the harbour waters? My enemy will say that the thief was not a thief and not a sailor but the son of a merchandising freed man, and that I insulted this son on the quayside and there was, in consequence, a brawl in which I killed a mere stripling. But this is not true, and whatever happened happened many years ago, so what care I about this idle tale? We are strong enough, you and I, to resist *that* threat.'

'So what will he try then, this enemy?'

'Threaten my body…threaten *you*…with torture.'

'But if we are soon to be dead anyway?'

'*You* are not soon to be dead. To be sure, you are sick; but not sick to death as I am. You see, you are the body to which I have chosen to return to make this request – that you will resist torture to save my poetry from being stolen.'

'But it cannot be stolen now. All the world – my world in my time – knows that the Second Eclogue was written by Publius Vergilius Maro: by Virgil.'

'But suppose I told you that unless you resist the torture that is coming to you, unless you (as my body) refuse to sign the document that swears away my poems, then, when you return to your own world in your own time, you will find a different name above these two poems?'

'I should not believe you. It is not possible.'

'Oh yes, it is. If some scholar of your era somehow found the document signed by you as my body, and therefore signed by us, or found a copy of it, he might "prove" to your world's satisfaction that I was not the true author of those poems. And so then, when you returned to your world or soon after you returned, you would see my poetry stolen from me.'

'*Never.*'

'Well spoken. Now get ready to resist.'

The door opened. Two pleasing young men, in full length togas, entered and sat down, one in either chair.

'Now, Virgil,' began the one on the left: 'you know very well who has sent us.'

'Some puking princelet, distant cousin to the August Caesar,' said Jeremy, finding the knowledge of this in his head and speaking it out, in his own voice, unprompted.

'Not so puking but that he could make what is left of your life a very miserable affair,' said the second pleasing young man.

'I should complain to the August Caesar.'

'He has what he wants of you: *The Aeneid*. He is no longer concerned for you. You are on your own, Virgil.'

'I have friends, coming to Brundisium to meet me,' said Jeremy.

'They have been delayed. That has been seen to. They are still at least several hours' journey away.'

'I do not believe you. Friends on such a mission do not brook delay easily. Anyhow, I shall sign or swear to nothing. Tell what stories you will of murders on quaysides.'

'Our patron knows well enough,' said the young man on the left, 'that that cock will not fight for him. He is, by the way, reducing his demand. He requires you to cede to him only the second Pastoral Poem –'

' – Never – '

' – And not the poem about Silenus. Just the one, he thinks, will be enough to make him immortal.'

There was a long silence. One of the oil-skinned figures walked down to the window and returned.

'No sign of your friends, you see,' said the youth on the right. 'Come along now, Virgil: you must know what will happen if you go on refusing. *We need your signature.* Forging it would be no good, because the August Caesar would detect the forgery and refuse the new attribution.'

'I thought you said that the August Caesar was no longer concerned with me.'

'He is still concerned, not with *you*, but with the work of the poet Publius Vergilius Maro – the author of *The Aeneid* which Caesar prizes so much. He would not allow that body of work to be diminished by having one of Virgil's minor but more exquisite poems attributed to somebody else – unless he knew for a certainty that the attribution was genuine.'

'It can never be genuine.'

'It can appear to be so, beyond any reasonable doubt, if once we have your signature assigning authorship to our patron.'

'Which you will never get.'

'Very well.'

The young man on the left produced an iron bar of perhaps half a yard in length and, in section, of half an inch in diameter. He began to heat it in the flambeau carried by the oil-skinned figure behind him. The other youth rose from his chair and turned Jeremy, bulky as he was, gently and deftly on to his belly.

'You can die like this, or in peace,' said the youth.

They will not kill me, thought Jeremy, because if they did I could not give them the 'genuine' signature which they need. They will frighten me, hurt me a bit, but they will not kill me…not unless they lose hope altogether. Now then: when Virgil dies, or rather when his spirit leaves me, I shall return to my own world. So much Virgil himself has said. If I can resist until Virgil leaves me, then I shall have won. But how can Virgil die and leave me if I am his body and, despite this fever, so strong? Or perhaps I am not so strong; perhaps the fever is killing me, and Virgil with it, after all. Yet Virgil has said this is not so. Then perhaps –

' – Don't let them steal my poem,' whispered the voice of Virgil in his ear. 'Defend my poem, Jeremy Morrison. Please.'

Just as the oil-skinned figures had not heard Virgil's voice earlier, so the two young emissaries did not appear to hear it now.

'I think,' said one of them, 'just a touch between the legs to start with.'

Jeremy screamed and screamed at the appalling pain.

'Don't let them steal my poem, you that have loved it.'

The pain again. And when he had stopped screaming,

'Sign now, and it will all be over.'

'NEVER.'

'Brave body, to resist so long and bear so much, all for my poem.'

'I love your poem and you. I shall defend you both.'

'A little further in this time,' said the youth on the right. 'Don't overdo it; just a little further in.'

But now both the oil-skinned figures were at the window waving their flambeaux in answer to the lights that flared from below. There was a great clatter of horses and wheels, much shouting.

'Our friends,' said Virgil: 'thank you, brave body.'

The two youths rose and slunk through the door.

'Virgil,' came the shout from below: 'we have come to greet you with our love on your return.'

But Jeremy knew that Virgil was now gone.

'You greet me for the last time,' Jeremy shouted back.

The oil-skinned figures turned down their flambeaux.

'Virgil is dead,' came a murmuring from below; then a chant of triumph: 'but his poems will live forever.'

I did not yield, Jeremy thought: when I return to my world and my time, the Second Eclogue will still be Virgil's.

Then, again, the dark.

'Jeremy is in hospital,' said Fielding Gray to Piero and Marius, who had found No Name in the yacht harbour at Brindisi, and Fielding with it. 'He is not seriously ill. Just a fever and some sort of enteric chill – probably caught from getting soaked in a storm the other day. Funny business, though: we were walking up that quay last night when we were both seized and hustled into a passageway. Then... Jeremy and our assailants just vanished, and I was left alone. I reported it to the Italian Police, who were just interested enough to take down the details – and they came to the Jolly early this morning to say that Jeremy had been found, unconscious, on the steps of the Hospital. No sign of ill treatment, they said. I've been to see him. He doesn't really know what happened – thinks he must have been delirious from fever. He'd had some peculiar dream. Rather wonderful, he seemed to think. "And that settles it, Fielding," he said: "I have come to the Isles of the Blest and met the man whom, of all men, I would wish to meet. We have spoken together." "Spoken of what?" said I. "Spoken of what a man must live by. And now I shall go home." '

'He's decided absolutely?' Piero said.

'Yes. Our mission is over, it seems. Certainly he appears to be very happy with…with whatever he saw and heard. In time, he says, we may be able to write of it. But not quite yet.'

'Do you think Carmilla will be satisfied?'

'Oh yes,' said Fielding. 'You've only got to look at him. Weak as he is from this enteric thing, he has been transformed into a kind of seer or prophet. He has the look of a man who has seen and spoken with God. Carmilla must surely settle for that. She should be very happy.'

Raisley Conyngham was not at all happy.

'Jeremy's decision had been made,' he said to Milo Hedley, 'before Marius ever saw him, before Marius and Caspar even arrived in Brindisi. And Marius knew this: Fielding Gray had told him. So Marius had no part in Jeremy's experience or decision – no part whatever. He did not even have to determine whether or not he should try to influence Jeremy, or what words to use. There would have been no point. Marius was totally cut out of the whole business from the moment Fielding told him that Jeremy was in hospital and had taken an absolute decision to return home, having now set foot on the Islands of the Blessèd and been vouchsafed his vision.'

'So we shall have to wait until the next time,' said Milo. 'Have you seen Marius?'

'He came to report to me. He was rather dazed. I think he felt that he had been let off.'

'What would he have done if he hadn't been let off?'

'He *says* that he would have urged Jeremy to come home, as we wished. Perhaps he would have. Obviously that Caspar had been getting at him, trying to swing him over to *their* side, but I don't know how much difference that would have made…had it come to the test. But it didn't. As you say, Milo, we shall just have to wait until next time. Anyway, Marius has now gone off to that old woman by the sea in Somerset. Have you seen Jeremy?'

'Not a glimpse. Not a squeak. Whatever happened to Jeremy does not seem to have helped my cause much.'

'All very frustrating. It's high time something went right for us. No good whining, however. Happy New Year…dear Milo.'

They raised their glasses to each other across the table.

'Jeremy was feverish,' said Carmilla to Theodosia and the rest that were assembled at Canteloupe's for the Twelve Days of Christmas – that was Canteloupe himself, Balbo Blakeney, Leonard Percival, Teresa (Tessa) Malcolm, Giles Glastonbury, Piero Caspar and Fielding Gray. 'Fielding will tell you how they weathered a ghastly storm and spent the night soaked through in one of those *Trulli* things by the shore. Jeremy was tired and shocked so they picked him up on the quay and doped him – '

' – They?'

'Two assistants whom Derek Mannering found. Twins apparently…who bore a disconcerting resemblance to the Helmutt twins, twelve-year-old faces, sixteen-year-old physique. They kept an eye on Jeremy and Fielding until they reached Brindisi. Then they kidnapped Jeremy and handed him over to Derek Mannering, who's a very fine actor when he chooses but is so bloody minded he's usually "resting", and to Doctor La Soeur, who knows a thing or two about hypnosis and these days is much at leisure for such exploits. So. Given superb acting by Derek as the Voice of Virgil and in the double role (all done by mirrors) of the two villains of the piece, and given La Soeur's skill at suggesting things to people that are drugged and provoking acute bodily reactions with harmless stimuli – there you have it. The Death of Virgil. Jeremy's Vision and his Test. Of course he decided to come home after it – as I very much hoped he would when I wrote the script. And of course there was no chance whatever for Marius to get at him or betray him. Quite how Marius now stands over this, I don't yet know. I shall possibly find out when I see him next week at Auntie Flo's.'

'What shall you do about the twins?' asked Balbo.

'Nothing. It's not absolutely certain that they're the Helmutt twins. Whoever they are, they seem entirely happy, according to Derek and La Soeur. And now they've simply vanished. So there's no point in alerting or bothering Marigold. Incidentally, however, since they won't talk to anyone, the odds are that they probably *are* the Helmutts. And for another thing, they seemed very attached to Jeremy. I suppose they used to see him when they were younger and he was at Cambridge, and they associate him with what they had of a childhood.'

'Where is Jeremy?' said Tessa.

'Celebrating the New Year with his father at Luffham, to the great pleasure of their potty old servant.'

'Well,' said Fielding Gray. 'Well, well.' Clearly audible through the open window, the Bell, Old Mortality, struck from the Campanile. 'Here's to a Happy – and Wholesome New Year,' said Fielding. 'The old one hasn't ended too badly.'

On the eleventh stroke the chime faltered, to be followed, on the twelfth, by the hideous grinding of the giant clapper on riven metal.

Walmer: Corfu: Castellonet de la Conquista: Florence.
March 21, 1988

SIMON RAVEN

MORNING STAR

This first volume in Simon Raven's *First-born of Egypt* saga opens with the christening of the Marquess Canteloupe's son and heir, Sarum of Old Sarum. The ceremony, attended by the godparents and the real father, Fielding Gray, is not without drama.

The christening introduces a bizarre cast of eccentric characters and complicated relationships. In *Morning Star* we meet the brilliant but troublesome teenager Marius Stern. Marius' increasingly outrageous behaviour has him constantly on the verge of expulsion from prep school. When his parents are kidnapped, apparently without reason, events take a turn for the worse.

THE FACE OF THE WATERS

This is the second volume of Simon Raven's *First-born of Egypt* series. Marius Stern, the wayward son of Gregory Stern, has survived earlier escapades and is safely back at prep school – assisted by his father's generous contribution to the school's new shooting-range. Fielding Gray and Jeremy Morrison are returning home via Venice, where they encounter the friar, Piero, an ex-male whore and a figure from a shared but distant past.

Back in England, at the Wiltshire family home, Lord Canteloupe is restless. He finds his calm disturbed by events: the arrival of Piero; Jeremy's father's threat to saddle his son with the responsibility of the family estate; and the dramatic resistance of Gregory Stern to attempted blackmail.

SIMON RAVEN

BEFORE THE COCK CROW

This is the third volume in Simon Raven's *First-born of Egypt* saga. The story opens with Lord Canteloupe's strange toast to 'absent friends'. His wife Baby has recently died and Canteloupe has been left her retarded son, Lord Sarum of Old Sarum. This child is not his, but has been conceived by Major Fielding Gray. In Italy there is an illegitimate child with a legitimate claim to the estate, whom Canteloupe wants silenced.

The plot also sees young Marius Stern and his school friend, Tessa Malcolm, drawn into Milo Hedley's schemes and into a dramatic finale orchestrated by Raisley Conyngham, Milo's teacher.

NEW SEED FOR OLD

The fourth in the *First-born of Egypt* series has Lord Canteloupe wanting a satisfactory heir so that his dynasty may continue. Unfortunately, Lord Canteloupe is impotent and his existing heir, little Tully Sarum, is not of sound mind.

His wife Theodosia is prepared to do her duty when a suitable partner is found. Finding the man and the occasion proves somewhat tricky, however, and it is not until Lord Canteloupe goes up to Lord's for the first match of the season that progress is made.

'Raven's unique vision of our times – classes battling,
corruption raging, ideas flashing – is not only valid, but
valuable. He spins webs of chance, intrigue and wit to ensnare
civilised values and trap the truth'
– *Mail on Sunday*

SIMON RAVEN

IN THE IMAGE OF GOD

The sixth in the *First-born of Egypt* series sees Raisley Conyngham, Classics teacher at Lancaster College, Cambridge, exert a powerful influence over Marius Stern. His young pupil, however, is no defenceless victim.

Marius has a ruthless streak and an ability to sidestep tests and traps that are laid for him. Which is just as well because everybody is after something from him...

'Raven's world of upper- and upper-middle-class mores, or amores more like, is outrageous and funny, elegant and sharp'
– *The Times*

AN INCH OF FORTUNE

'Presuming even your capacity for borrowing money without qualm or security has by now lost much of its edge, it only remains that you should make some.'

The words of the Bursar ringing in his ears, Esme Sangrail Sa Foy is pushed into working in his summer holidays as a way of settling his college's bills. Hired by the Honourable Mrs Sandra Fairweather, as holiday tutor to her adopted son Terence, Esme's brief is unusual. Not expected to teach Terence anything, he is there to keep him out of trouble.

Perhaps Terence's psychiatrist Doctor MacTavish is a sign that nothing in the Fairweather household is what it seems. As the summer develops and Esme and Terence leave London for Suffolk and finally Biarritz, Esme makes his discoveries.

Printed in Great Britain
by Amazon.co.uk, Ltd.,
Marston Gate.